CW00481949

And Then
I Shall
Transform

Amy Laurens

Other Works

Find other works by the author at
www.amylaurens.com/books

AND THEN I SHALL
Transform

Amy Laurens

AUSTRALIA

Print ISBN: 978-1-922434-94-4
eBook ISBN: 9798223531722

www.inkprintpress.com

National Library of Australia Cataloguing-in-Publication Data
Laurens, Amy 1985—
And Then I Shall Transform
124 p.   cm.
ISBN: 978-1-922434-94-4
Inkprint Press, Canberra, Australia
1. Fiction—Fantasy—Contemporary 2. Fiction— Fairy Tales, Folk Tales, Legends & Mythology 3. Fiction—Fantasy—Collection & Anthologies 4. Fiction—Short Stories (single author)

Summary: Six fantasy stories about magical transformations and the importance of being yourself.

First Edition: April 2024

Cover design © Inkprint Press
Internal illustrations © Amy Laurens

Contents

In Which Leaves Are Common Sense

MOST PEOPLE THINK LEAVES FALL IN AUTUMN BECAUSE they die, fluttering drifts of red and yellow and orange and brown, twirling on a breeze that smells like the promise of ice before falling to skitter along the ground with a hollow tick-tick-tick.

Most people, it turns out, are wrong.

About many things of course, but in this case about the leaves: deciduous trees don't just shed their leaves wantonly, carelessly—or even regretfully.

No.

Deciduous trees lose their leaves because they are frugal.

Turns out, the only reason the leaves change colour in the first place—be that ruby or pumpkin, butternut or hazel, or some striated rainbow in between—is because the cooling weather lulls the plant into sleepiness, and a sleeping plant is a plant that can't eat (frozen leaves aren't much good at collecting sunlight anyway, not when frost bursts their cell walls like bubbles, sharp fragments of ice severing pathways like a knife through warm, fresh neurons).

The colour change is just the outward signal of the tree's common sense: drawing back in all the nutrients the leaf has to offer, slurping them back into the trunk where the tree can nurse on them all winter long, shedding the now-empty leaves like scales, sloughing them off like old skin, discarding dead storage units until the risk of frostbite has passed.

The day I realised I could do the same changed my life.

THE SNOW WAS—PREDICTABLY—COLD. IT WAS ALSO early, and I'd been caught out hiking unprepared, which was just about the dumbest thing I'd managed to do yet in my life—apart from, maybe, George, and also attending New Beat University. An avid hiker since I'd been old enough to carry any sort of day pack with my parents, I knew the risks inside and out, backward and forward, upside and down.

Never go hiking alone.

Always pack extra Puritabs.

Let people know where you're going, and when you expect to be back.

Take warmer things than you think you'll need.

No one gives advice on what to do when your hike-mate has a sudden attack of lunar-cy, though, three days before the full moon. No one tells you what to do when you're abruptly alone in a sea of grey-trunked eucalypt trees and tea tree scrub that stinks like face cleanser and scratches like the blazes, and you've now got two packs' worth of gear to hike out. Alone.

Werewolves are not considerate hiking buddies, let me be the first to assure you.

Well. Amendment: Probably some of them are, maybe even most of them.

George? Not so much.

(In hindsight, unsurprising: he'd never been a very considerate roommate, either, no matter what physical form he was in.)

And, of course, it was cold.

And as I stood in the clearing where considerate wildlife had trampled down the tussock grass and a fallen gum tree was busy turning silver as it weathered, cold air singeing the inside of my nostrils and burning the tip of my nose, I realised I had a choice: I could get really, *really* cold as I sat around waiting for George to human up again—probably in three or four days once the moon had passed, but then again, he wasn't supposed to have wolfed out this earlier either, so who knew?—or I could get really really warm trying to hike two packs' worth of gear back out.

Or—I scratched my nose, face screwed up—I could redistribute the gear, take the expensive or vital stuff out in one pack, leave the rest somewhere covered and come back when it was safe.

With someone other than George, of course.

Bloody George.

I sighed heavily, rolled my pack over onto its back like a floundering sea lion, and began unbuckling the straps. Stupid to think I could hike a whole day out with both full packs. Not worth the risk.

The sky told me what it thought of that: the clouds that had been fitfully scudding across the sky coagulated into something thick and soupy and so low it seemed like I could practically touch it (or at least throw something high enough to touch it, like a rock, or maybe George, who deserved to be tossed into the sky) and the sky began to spit at me.

I rolled my eyes at the melodrama, rustled the brim of my cherry-red raincoat down over my forehead, and set about repacking the packs.

Out came my bag of dirty clothes. Would I regret leaving them if I needed extra warmth? Probably not.

Stupid weather, sky-spit freezing my fingers and making them slow.

Sleeping mat. Ditched. I had one night max to spend outdoors, and that was if I spent the rest of today lollygagging around instead of moving at pace.

Stupid moon, exerting whatever stupid influence it was over stupid werewolves at a stupid time of the month.

Sleeping bag.

Well. Obviously I was going to hold onto that one, just in case.

Only one though. George could keep his own furry butt warm if it came to that.

Food—check, definitely coming with. Compass, maps, cook stove—yes, yes and yes.

Tent. Obviously. Just in case.

Dammit. I'd have to take both halves.

I fished the fly and poles out of George's pack and rammed them into my own.

The sky stopped spitting and started snowing at me, frigid air turning my fingers red, the scent of the bush subtly shifting from eucalypt to wet grass and now to snow itself.

The hell.

It was March. Yes, okay, fine, it was autumn by the calendar, but the last five, ten years March had grown *hot*. Like, summer hot. No one reasonably expected even a sudden transient fit of cold weather until April, which was why I'd agreed to this hike with George in the first place.

A cold snap? Sure. Unfortunate, but this wasn't our first hike in the bush and we'd brought layers.

Snow?

What. The actual. Hell.

I scowled at the steely clouds, shoved the last of the necessities into my pack, and drew the drawstring tight around its neck.

Flipped the lid of the pack shut, canvas scuffing loudly in the silence of the bush. Snapped the buckles shut—snap, snap, echoing around the clearing.

A third snap.

I froze.

My pack definitely only had two buckles to close, and George's pack was right there in front of me, wallowing on the ground like an unholy grey hippopotamus.

My ears tried to crawl off my head as I tried to surveil the bush around me without appearing to.

...A rustle, perhaps? Behind and to my left, where the gum trees thinned in both density and girth and the spiky, pale tussock grass traced a path down a gentle slope to a green hollow largely occupied by a white cedar of impressive height.

The dang berries on the cedar were toxic. I knew that. George knew that. But did George's lunar form know that?

I may or may not have let my pack fall sideways with a bit of firm assistance as I swore and clambered to my feet.

Definitely a rustle, that now became a susurrus of disturbed grass as something grey and the size of a large kangaroo or a small wolf vanished into the teatree scrub.

I ground my teeth. Inhaled icy-cold air. Buried my hands under my armpits and cursed past-me momentarily for not packing gloves, summer-like weather be damned. Then I trudged after the critter toward the hollow.

The white cedar gleamed like a golden crown amid the grey-and-olive eucalypts, framed above by the grey sky, its buttery autumn leaves flipping and fluttering in a breeze no other tree seemed to feel.

And underneath it, George: a grey wolf resting on his haunches with a wide, doggy grin on his face, tongue lolling to one side.

"George," I said sternly, "I have too far to hike today to be messing around anymore with you. Either get your butt back here and let me strap a pack to your furry hide, or leave me alone so I can get home without losing my fingers to frostbite."

I burrowed my hands deeper into my armpits, which probably would have been more effective if I'd had them under my raincoat, but that would mean opening said raincoat, which, no.

As if sensing the nearness of the end of my emotional tether, the sky very kindly hit pause on the whole snow situation.

My nose still burned with the cold.

"On second thoughts, get your furry butt over here so I can bury my face in it for a moment and warm up." My nose wrinkled. "Your fur, that is, I'm not burying my face in your butt."

George's grin didn't budge. He'd told me before that he had a hard time remembering how language worked while he was a wolf, but I squinted at him nonetheless.

"If you laugh, I'll murder you on the spot."

Happy panting.

Heaving a sigh to end all sighs, rolling my eyes hard enough that even Temporary Wolf Boy couldn't fail to read my emotions, I stomped back to the clearing where I'd left the packs.

The packs were gone.

For the splittiest of seconds, I froze again—and then because I was actually starting to freeze, I strode to the spot where the packs had lain, thin rapiers of grass still crushed and buckled in their wake, and howled, "George!!"

To his credit, he appeared almost instantly at the fringe of the clearing again, peering out between the gnarled and twisted fingers of the tea tree.

"Where," I said, "are our packs?" As if staring at him sternly with my hands on my hips would suddenly spur him to speech.

I ground my teeth.

The clouds hung above, not even a little movement in them to indicate the passing of time, no glimpse of the sunlight we'd been expecting shining through. Surely it was at least mid-morning now though, and I had, what, six hours to hike out to safety?

Fine.

Fine, I'd do it without George, without the packs—and without water I realised with a sinking stomach.

Okay.

Okay fine.

That would suck, but it was six hours, maybe seven or eight if I took it really slow to conserve energy, and sunset wasn't until... I narrowed my eyes. *I don't know, maybe five thirty, six o'clock? It was twilight when I was sitting down to dinner on Tuesday and that was...*

Sure, sunset was maybe six o'clock if I was lucky.

So I had six, maybe eight hours to walk on six, maybe seven, possibly eight hours of daylight.

Easy.

Absolutely plausible.

And it was freezing, so no doubt I'd drink less anyway. Ah ha. Ah ha-ha ha ha.

At least I'd walk faster without a pack.

THE SECOND TIME I CAME ACROSS THE WHITE CEDAR IN THE hollow, I swore loudly enough that I disturbed a pair of magpies fossicking around in the dirt. They flapped and squawked back at me, perching up on a tea tree branch just above my head and giving me the indignant eye.

Much as I was *so sorry* to have interrupted their lunch, I was far more worried about the tree.

Butter yellow, still shivering as though it could feel the cold as well as I could—and *bloody George* sitting right beneath it, grinning at me.

"George," I said in a perfectly reasonable tone, "what the actual."

He whuffed, wagged his tail twice as though domestication had already sunk its claws into him, and watched me stomp out of the hollow, footsteps heavy with boots that weren't doing enough to preserve the circulation in my slowly numbing toes.

The magpies squawked happily as I left and fluttered back to the ground to look for lunch.

My stomach rumbled.

THE THIRD TIME I CAME ACROSS THE TREE, I SAID NOTHING, just scowled at it, at George, at the pair of magpies still busy aerating petrichorish soil, and stomped away with the tasted of dirt and damp bark in my palate.

THE FOURTH TIME, I SIGHED, SHAMBLED OVER TO THE granite boulder that crouched, lichen-spattered, beneath the cedar, and sat. "What's going on?" I asked George.

He rested his chin over my legs, wet-dog-gone-feral temporarily out-competing wet tea tree for my olfactory real estate.

I grimaced. "You're disgusting."

He licked my face.

I squealed, wiped slobber from my cheek with a nearly numb hand, and scowled again. "I'm just trying to get out alive," I told him. "Why do you-and-or-this-tree have such a problem with that?"

He didn't answer, but apparently the sky had a problem with it too, because now it began to snow in earnest.

Snow in Australia isn't *pretty* like you see in other places. I presume it falls in flakes because that's what science tells me, but if it does, they're far too small to make out. It mostly just looks like sleet, like tiny white specks that might be rain if not for the fact that the wind blows them sideways just a little too easily, and that occasionally, they flurry.

I guess for some people it might still count as pretty.

I guess I'm not some people.

Even the magpies decided to pack it in, launching themselves into the air and swooping featherily away.

If only.

Instead, I was stuck in the slowly freezing bush, apparently doing circles with neither food nor water nor warmth, and at any point now the sun was going to start its inevitable decline from the zenith somewhere behind those clouds, and before I knew it, I'd be foodless and waterless and warmthless *in the dark*.

George whined.

"What?" I snapped. "What do I have to do? I can't just magic myself into a warm coat like you can, you know."

Idly, I wondered if that was exactly what he'd done; had he—or even just his body, his subconscious—had some sort of warning about what was going to happen, and this was his body's way of dealing with it?

Where the *hell* had the packs gone?

I leaned over, buried my face in the musky wet fur of George's ruff, and may or may not have cried.

Only then I realised that was wasting water, *and* it was making my face wet i.e. cold, so I performed an extremely inelegant face-wipe against George's fur that I expressly forbade him ever to mention, and sat up with a horribly shaky inhale.

It was still snowing.

I still had no packs.

But probably there was something to the theory that crying was your body's way of purging excess emotions, because I did indeed feel calmer.

Calm enough that I closed my eyes, tilting my face up to the underside of the white cedar's canopy. The air was still, and quiet, the kind of quiet you only get with snow.

George was warm on my lap.

The cedar's trunk was more or less at my back, and if I slumped just a little, like so, it was shaped just right to cradle me.

A momentary wind gusted past, and even though my eyes were already closed, I squinted against the cold.

A cedar berry boinked me on my nose.

I wrinkled my nose.

My breathing slowed.

Eh.

If I was going to die here, at least there were worse ways to go.

I'd always heard that hypothermia was a weird one, where you got colder and colder and sleepier and sleepier until suddenly, right at the end, you got a burst of warmth, and felt suddenly so hot you wanted to strip all your clothes off, shed all the excess layers that you didn't need anymore because you'd drawn all their warmth into yourself, and you had everything you needed from them, and could discard them like the useless, empty vessels that they were.

I shucked out of my raincoat.

It slithered nylonly to the ground.

Boots. My boots were big and hot and heavy, anchoring my feet to the ground. They were hard to unlace, though, and harder still to lace back up.

I stayed where I was against the trunk and let my feet sink into the ground, just like George was sinking into my lap and I was sinking into the tree behind me.

Oh.

I hadn't realised hallucinations were part of hypothermia as well, but it really did feel like I was sinking into the tree, my arms rising slowly to meld into the branches, my spine lengthening toward the steel-grey sky, my heart slowing as my blood pulsed in time with the sap.

I smiled.

Wood creaked.

George whined softly.

I tried to pet him, to reassure him that it was okay, I didn't mind dying like this, that maybe now the university would stop hassling me about my parking fees and the dean of boarding would quit complaining that our dorm room stank of dog because—didn't we know—there were "No pets allowed on campus," we chorused together for the millionth time, in the deep-fried cafeteria, in the cigarette-smoke pavilion, on the creek-water bridge where the ducklings came to try their hand —wing—feet?—at swimming, and...

And, well, I couldn't well pat my wolf friend with *branches* for arms, now could I. Hmm. That wouldn't do.

I opened my mouth—knothole—mouth—what was I doing?

My sap hummed happily up and down my phloem, and my toes—roots? Yes, roots, they wriggled happily in the soil, chatting chemically with the cedar whose roots entwined my own, warning of a nematode outbreak on the up-sun side at the furthermost extent of our reach.

I shivered.

Yellow leaves drifted away in the wind.

ALL CREATURES, IT TURNS OUT, HAVE THEIR OWN FORM OF common sense. We can't always access it—sometimes we're numbed to it by circumstance or choice—but when we do?

I smiled, caressing the trunk of the cedar who'd once been a woman. She'd turned in the depths of a snap far colder than mine, had had to clothe herself in bark and arboreal frugality much longer in order to survive—until now, she had only one choice: remain a tree, or die.

I could think of worse things.

I was still glad the weather had warmed after only a day or two for me, my soft body slowly returning to itself, disorientation at having to remember how to speak with my mouth and not my extremities, how to breathe through a single, inefficient appendage instead of with every pore of my skin leaving me frozen in place as the sun's long fingers crept across the grassy green hollow, the warmth baking tea tree into the air.

George was still a wolf. The full moon probably hadn't passed.

But this time, as I rose stiffly to my feet and hefted the grey pack onto my back that had somehow always been resting just there at the periphery of the white cedar's reach, George stayed with me. And he kept staying with me, the whole way back to the car, which he'd never done before as a wolf because he told me humans stank too much to live with when you had about fifty times more scent receptors than your average nose-blind human.

So maybe George wasn't the biggest mistake I ever made.

And maybe—though it's truly bizarre to con-sider—neither was getting caught out in early snow, effectively hiking alone, unprepared for whatever it was that was just about to happen.

Tims Testing Day

Hot CHIPS WITH THE SLIGHTLY VINEGAR TANG OF ketchup: that was the prevailing scent of the Tim Group cafeteria. On Thursdays, it was replaced by the tomato paste, sweet-acidic, caramelised savoury smell of spag bol, and occasionally on the weekend a fishy flavour lingered. But for the most part, the hot chips-and-ketchup prevailed.

It wasn't because there was nothing else to be had at the caf, nor even that there was nothing healthy; in fact, for the most part, the food there was entirely healthy—but salads are rather lacking in scents distinctive and strong enough to compete with the chips, so the chips won out.

Tim wasn't the least bit bothered by this, because, to his mind, it was always a good day for chips. Well, thus he'd always proclaimed, loudly and seriously to anyone who would listen—usually detractors and disputers, of course.

But today, his stomach was trying to turn him liar. Flipping and twisting, it was doing its best impersonation of a queasy eel—which idly reminded Tim of the story he'd heard about intestines having to be hung up on hooks during bowel surgeries because of their tendency to writhe around in that peculiarly brainless muscular fashion shared by beheaded snakes and lizard-less tails, all of which did spectacularly little to enable Tim to keep the idea of food in mind without wanting to bring up empty-stomach bile.

He pressed a hand firmly against his stomach in an attempt to still it, and inched forward in the metres-long queue.

"You 'kay?" another Tim asked from behind, a tall, muscular fellow with broad shoulders and a somewhat scraggly beard.

Tim shrugged. "Yeah. I'm fine."

"Testing day, right?" the bearded Tim asked with a sympathetic half-smile.

"Yeah."

"You'll be fine," Tim said. "Barely anyone drops out by testing stage."

"I know." He did know. He knew all the stats.

Twenty-six percent of applications accepted.

Sixty-three percent of those advanced to the second month of training.

A further forty-two percent weeded out over the next eleven months in the Tim Group Compound.

That left five of them out of the forty-nine who'd first applied twelve months ago. Statistically speaking, only one of them would fail testing. But Tim was too conservative for one-in-five odds to ever feel better than random chance.

"It's nothing you haven't already been doing," Tim said in a voice that was clearly trying to offer more information than the words themselves—but Tim was at a complete loss as to what the other Tim was hinting at.

Still. "I know," he said.

His mouth was dry, now. Eely stomach and dry mouth and oh, heck, his heart was starting to pound now and the test wasn't even for—he checked his green plastic wristwatch—another five minutes.

The lunch queue moved forward, the hum and bub of general chatter ebbing and flowing across the large space of the cafeteria, designed to seat a hundred and currently a little over capacity. (It had been a good couple of years for Tims, he knew that too: most annual cohorts bore only two or three successful Tims, and the last four years had seen five to eight apiece.)

Who knew. Maybe Tim'd get lucky and all five of them would pass.

He looked at his wristwatch again. Four minutes nineteen seconds.

The queue moved forward.

That was the worst of it, he decided. The being told to go about their business as though nothing was happening. 'Ignore the test,' the instructors had said. 'It'll come when it comes, and you can't prepare, no special equipment needed, so you might as well be doing whatever it is you'd usually be doing when it happens.'

Of course, he wasn't supposed to *know* when the test was going to occur, right down to the second. But bearded Tim wasn't the only sympathetic heart in the Group.

Tim wondered if the others in their cohort had been similarly prepared.

A mindless step forward, and then—"Hmm? Oh, yes, just the chips thanks. No, no salad. No ketchup, thank you."

A siren screamed across the cafeteria.

Tim fumbled his tray, nearly dropped it entirely.

Ketchup splashed the floor.

"TIM!" someone shrieked from the main doorway. "HELP!"

Tim dropped the tray properly this time and sprinted.

So did everyone else in the cafeteria.

As one, a room full of Tims pelted toward the person screaming in the doorway, who turned at the sight of the onslaught and rabbited.

The horde of Tims followed, adrenaline pumping hard in Tim's veins, thrilling through his limbs, singing in his lungs.

This. This was what he'd been born for.

The chase wound through the complex for a few lung-burning minutes before the rabbit—a woman with long blonde hair pulled back into a tight braid, a stranger to the compound—led them to a halt at the Tree.

Four storeys high with largely bare, sprawling grey branches and leaves reminiscent of a fig's, if fig leaves grew to the size of dinner plates, the Tree stood at the sacred heart of the complex—and right next to the cafeteria, practically back where they'd begun.

Six months ago, Tim would have resented the pointless interval of the run, would've been leaning over his legs gasping and clutching at his side. But six months' training had done their job: Tim stood tall, breathing a little faster than usual perhaps but no more discernibly winded than any other Tim in the group. And so, he was able to watch with eager interest, undistracted by simple things like oxygen consumption and stitches, as the Tree began to glow.

It was a faint green to begin with, deepening slowly to rich gold.

Tim'd heard that it did that, sometimes, but that was all he'd heard: it wasn't a thing one spoke of with novices, apparently.

And now, here he was, *experiencing* it.

Excitement thrilled through him, not too dissimilar to the adrenaline it displaced. His hands were suddenly tacky with sweat, and it was hard not to bounce a little on his toes as the golden glow of the tree expanded, washing over the crowd.

With it, a sense of peace like nothing Tim'd ever experienced. A sense of *right*ness.

He'd thought while running, caught up in the frenzied joy of the mob, that *that* was what he'd been born to do.

He was wrong.

This was what he was meant to do.

Bathe in the luxurious, calming glow of the Tree as its magic gently warmed him.

He felt it settle into his bones, a soul-deep shift of microscopic proportions and infinite significance.

Felt the magic burn, not like a searing, awful heat, but like sunshine that warmed him from the inside out.

Felt the collective minds of the Tims gathered together into the Tree as though they were merely all branches of the same single organism, which was the purpose of the magic of the Tree: to bind all Tims together, to make them effectively one person, so that the magic that had been gifted to the very first Tim—and to that first Tim alone— would recognise them all.

Tim lifted his hands. Stared wide-eyed as the glow emanating now from his fingers.

Wriggled a little—experimentally, with buoy-chested delight.

The dark-haired Tim on their right nudged him. "Your first time?"

He nodded, stripped wordless with wonder, with peace, with the weight of the thoughts and emotions of all the other Tims pressing softly against him.

The dark-haired Tim smiled knowingly. "Congratulations."

Tim's eyebrows twitched at that. Congratulations? But... The test? Had that been...

He blinked. He'd been expecting something... difficult? Challenging? Unfamiliar?

But this...

The person had called, and he had answered—partly from twelve long months of reconditioning himself to answer to the new name, to forget his deadname, to absorb and inhabit his new identity entirely—but partly because it had been so... *easy.*

Tim was who he *was.*

Answering was what he was called to *do.*

He followed, because that was what he'd been *born* for.

Behind them, whispers rippled.

Something about the tone caught at his ear; something furtive, a tension at odds with the peace of the Tree's magical golden glow.

Tim turned with the Tims around them—and the whole crowd was parting, drawing back, and Tim could feel the growing horror in the air as the whole Group shrank back from one person on their fringe, one person who was still leaning over their thighs and gasping a little, staring up anxiously as everyone avoided their eye contact.

The person—youngish, shortish brownish hair, tannish skin, girlish, if that mattered—hunched in on themselves. "What?" the person said. "What is it?"

But Tim knew.

Tim had never seen this before, had never undergone the test before, had never been part of the

most intimate, magical heart of the Tim Group...
but he knew.

This person shying away from the collective
gaze of the group?

They were not glowing.

They were not a Tim.

Somehow, they had not answered fast enough,
or thoroughly enough, or else it had just simply
never been meant to be—and they had failed the
test.

"I'm so sorry, Jen," said the nearest Tim, a tall,
gangly Tim with long, silky red hair, putting an arm
around the ex-prospective Tim.

Jen.

Jen.

Tim hadn't known the prospective Tim's deadname. Hearing it now, after twelve months living
exclusively with a hundred other Tims, discom-
forted them in a way too deep for words.

It wasn't fair.

But the first bargain had never been meant to
be fair.

*A seed of plant magic for Tim, in exchange for
services rendered.*

That was what was engraved on the plaque at
the base of the Tree, what had been engraved on
the seed the Tree had grown from, a gift to the very
first Tim from none other than the High Wood Fae
themselves.

And Tim, the very first Tim, had wrung every
drop of meaning from that gift that he possibly

could. Plant magic, gifted from the fae, had allowed him to develop a thriving business maintaining rich people's gardens with nary the touch of a finger; his cunning had allowed him to develop a legacy when he'd realised he could convince the magic that it applied to anyone who shared the Tim identity.

Only eight percent of applicants were able to sink deeply enough into the Tim identity for the Tree to accept them. Only eight percent of applicants were able to shed their old lives fully enough that no trace of it remained.

Only eight percent of applicants, Tim suspected, really *wanted* to shed their old identities fully enough.

The other ninety-two percent *thought* they did... But the proof was in the judgement of the Tree.

It was sad for Jen, of course. But Tim would be lying if he didn't admit that the peace of the Tree—the peace of belonging, of acceptance—wasn't washing that sorrow quickly away.

Jen would find their own place in time. Nearly everybody did.

Tim turned back to the Tree—as were the other Tims, now—and smiled beatifically.

The instructors had been right all along: there was no way to prepare for a test when all it really did was see you for who you truly were.

Familiars Need Enrichment Too

IN CASTLE BOWELS THAT WOULD HAVE BEEN DEEP HAD IT not been for the fact that actually, they were at ground level, Bystar squished his nose hard up against the leadlight windows of the hidden room he'd spent more-or-less the last month trapped in and sighed wistfully. Out there, in the gradually unfurling spring, willows' long hair trailed in the dark waters of the moat, clouds teased through the gaps in the branches of the river red gums, and sunlight flickered as a brisk wind whipped over the city. Out there, Bystar knew, the world would smell of bitter pollen and sweet grass, cool eucalypt and the bitter scent of the moat.

In here, the smell was best described as musty.

He sighed, sneezed as the breath puffed up more of the dust that had, despite his spending four weeks sloughing along the windowsill, gathered there again, and twitched a rounded ear.

"Come down from there, will you," Mercury muttered absently from her spot curled up in the dark green armchair.

For a moment, Bystar considered slinking over to join her, burrowing into the warm crevasse between her body and the soft velveteen of the armchair, curling into a tight ball with his tail over his nose and sleeping his boredom away.

Halfheartedly, he raised a hind leg to scratch his stomach.

Relatively ineffectual, and Mercury would do a much better job of sating his itch were he to go throw himself on her lap and writhe around a bit, but... "I'm *booooored*," he wailed, nails clutching at the edge of the wooden windowsill. "Ferrets aren't supposed to be cooped up, I'm a wild animal. I need to get out! Stretch my legs!"

Mercury's eyebrow raised, but her eyes didn't leave the huge hardback she'd spent the last few days perusing. "Bystar, you're about as wild as a pug, so excuse me if my heart isn't exactly bleeding for you."

He lashed his tail, tan fur bristling. "Am too wild."

"Am not."

"Am too."

Mercury heaved a long-suffering sigh and closed her book, one finger marking her place. "Does it occur to you, ferret brain, that maybe I'm just as bored as you are?"

Yes. Cooped up in a tiny room just big enough for a bed, the armchair, and a floor-to-ceiling bookcase hiding the door, Bystar was well aware that he wasn't the only one growing dangerously bored around here. He narrowed his eyes at her—but there was no evidence of a storm cloud building directly over her head, a warning sign that she might be annoyed enough—*bored* enough—to start flicking tiny fireballs at his head for fun.

"Oh, stop cowering on the sill, I'm not going to throw a tantrum at you."

Bystar ran a clawed paw down his whiskers, a nervous-cum-thoughtful habit he couldn't quite remember when he'd picked up.

Which, he was not the only one picking up new habits: before their month-long confinement here in a hidden room of Deviran's castle—oops, don't think that one too loudly, that *would* be enough to send Mercury into a tantrum—Mercury would never had restrained herself from an opportunity to make her feelings loudly known to the room at large.

Restraint.

Not a word he'd ever expected to apply to Mercury.

He sighed dramatically and launched himself over the edge of the sill, plunging to the floor.

Mercury didn't move.

At the last second, he twisted around to land safely on his feet. Not a cat, don't ask him to perform that feat from a rooftop or anything, but from a four-foot windowsill he'd grown intimately, familiarly acquainted with?

He snapped at the dark green rug because he could, and slunk over to Mercury's chair.

Maybe he dug his claws in just a little harder than usual as he shinned up to her lap.

Didn't matter, though, because even then she didn't react, though it was possible that she hadn't noticed his claws through the thick denim she'd taken to wearing, but even *that* was an affront because how dare she wear clothing specifically designed to stop him from getting her attention.

He upended himself over her book, paws wriggling in the air, fluffy tail up against her shoulder.

She tickled his belly with an idle finger; he bit at it playfully. Or, well, playfully enough that she couldn't accuse him otherwise, anyway.

"Fine," he grouched. "I'm not a wild animal then. But if you're going to keep me as a pet, pets need enrichment." He practically whined the last word, scrabbling after her hand as she withdrew it. "Enrichment, Mercury! I'm feeling... I'm feeling... *un*enriched."

To her credit, Mercury didn't smile; her lips just quirked instead, her dark eyes glimmering. "Impoverished?"

"Yes, I'm feeling impoverished, and you might as well stop mocking me because I know you're feeling impoverished too." Bystar flicked himself back onto his feet and huffed with his back to her, something that probably would have been more effective if he hadn't still been on her lap.

If I say you can go for a wander, will you stop being a small black hole of negativity? Mercury's question landed directly in his head, a freakishly rare degree of Overlord-Familiar communication that Bystar half suspected was only possible because of Mercury's magical affinity for all things related to consciousness. *You're making it practically impossible to concentrate.*

On what? We've been stuck in this room for so long, all I can smell in here is me. Bystar took another fatalistic step from a moderate height, twisting as he got to the floor—and cracking his tail on the foot of the armchair as he landed. *Ow.*

"Not all of us," Mercury said aloud, resetting herself in her chair and opening the book back up, "are feeling impoverished. *Some* of us can read."

"Some of us can reeeaad..." Bystar mimicked, pulling a face and scowling up at her from the safety of the rug, her face out of sight.

I can still hear you though.

Bystar's scowl turned into bared teeth.

Fine, said Mercury. *I need to talk to Deviran anyway. Is an hour long enough?*

I don't know, is an hour long enough for you? Deep—very, very deep—down in the depths of his private thoughts, Bystar snickered. Mercury hated Deviran, current owner of the castle, oh yes. Hated him for publicly beating her for first place at the Evil Overlord Academy, hated him for saving her life, hated him for being right about the need for her to stay cooped up in the castle like this, pretending for all the world to be dead.

She hated him so much that, over the course of the last month, she'd started finding every excuse she could to hate him personally, and to his face. Three meals a day plus extra visits in between, and after every one of them she'd storm back to her room, thundercloud flashing and sparking over her head, stinking of anger—and lust.

Bystar snickered into his whiskers. *That* was certainly not a conversation he was going to wade into, enrichment, impoverished, or no.

Mercury snapped her book shut loudly and thudded her feet to the ground, narrowly missing not only Bystar's tail, but the rest of him as well.

He squeaked, scampered a few steps away, then reversed and shimmied up her denim-clad leg to haul himself up onto her shoulder.

"One hour," she said sternly as she pulled back the blue book on the case that clicked open the latch on the secret door. "That's all the enrichment we can afford right now. You may not be as well-known as I am, but someone is bound to get suspicious if they see you hanging around the castle too much."

Bystar nodded vigorously. "One hour."

Enrichment. Oh goodie.

REALLY, BYSTAR COULD HAVE LEFT THE CASTLE ANY TIME in the last four weeks. If he'd really wanted to. And if hard pressed—presumably up against a brick wall, in a corner, probably at knife point—for truth, he'd have to admit that it wasn't just a healthy respect for Mercury's tiny fireballs that had kept him confined.

Even though he could escape at any point without her, well, that was essentially the point: it would be without her, and that *didn't* seem to have a point.

Suffice to say, trotting along now down the wide gravel road that led from the castle alone was... odd. He flicked an ear irritably, sneezed at the bitter pollen wafting past nostrils not currently acclimated to anything except his own musk, and Mercury's honeysuckle scent, and the aged, musty smell of the castle.

Bystar glared at a magpie warbling its early spring song. *It* wasn't sitting there, worrying about whether its human would be alright for an hour without it. *It* wasn't having its joy at sudden and unexpected freedom dampened because it had to be out alone. *It* wasn't—

An overly large pebble pretending to be a small boulder forcibly interrupted Bystar's line of complaint.

Bystar scowled at it, shook his whiskers, ruffled out his fur... and took a quick steadying breath because there was no point wasting the entire hour being grumpy.

Score one for self-awareness. Mercury's dry voice drifted through his thoughts, and he winced.

Out here in the open air, with the wind in the gum trees and the sun flashing in and out of the clouds, he'd forgotten to keep such a tight hold on the shield around his thoughts. Whoops.

Ha ha, I'm fine... he thought loudly at Mercury, a tiny glimmer of pink somewhere deep in his subconscious.

Good. Then shut up and have fun. I'm still trying to concentrate.

Bystar sighed dramatically, his body wilting along the ground—and then he perked up, gathered himself, and trotted off in the general direction of the carriage stand, because really, what else was there to do.

ALMOST TWENTY MINUTES LATER, BYSTAR COULD THINK of plenty of better things to do that hadn't involved a long, boring walk which, when added to the long boring return walk, would take up most of his allotted hour.

Tail lashing, he stalked across the green grass— mercifully soft under his feet, unlike that pernicious gravel—he snarled at it for good measure —and paused at the fringe of spiky, white-flowered bushes that rimmed the carriage stand where four or five silvery, box-shaped carriages with large spoked wheels stood waiting to be engaged.

Carriages, hurrah.

Next stop: anywhere he wanted!

A tall man in a long woollen coat just a smidge too heavy for the spring weather emerged from the other side of the small square, hurried to a carriage, placed his palm on the window until it turned green, and climbed inside.

Blood and despair. Bystar sat heavily, curling his tail around him and squishing it in his front paws. Apparently he'd been cooped up for so long he'd forgotten how the carriages worked: automatic boxes on wheels, you could direct them anywhere you wanted in the city—if you were tall enough to reach the glass pane with a hand human enough for the pane to recognise.

Specie-ism. That's what this was. He scowled, then nibbled the end of his tail. *Now* what was he going to do? Give up and go ho—go back to the *castle*, that was?

The carriage the man had entered rumbled to life, vibrating gently in the square.

Bystar tilted his head.

Well. That was one solution...

He ran.

He leapt.

And as the silvered carriage puttered out of the dusty square, the sun flickered over a small tan ferret, hanging precariously from the moulding on the carriage's rear bumper.

WITH A JARRING THUD THAT RATTLED HIS TEETH, BYSTAR dropped to the dusty road, tucking and rolling for his life.

He'd wanted to stop here, right in front of the— he glanced up at a sign that bore curling gold letters on a black background and thought them hard at Mercury—*Ye Olde Analog Witch*, came the translation—yes, right in front of Ye Olde Analog Witch. That was *absolutely* where he'd been intending to visit, and anyone who said he'd only ended up here because his poor, cramped little paws couldn't hold onto the juddering bumper of the carriage a moment longer could go bite themselves. Hard.

Bystar limped into the shade cast by the witchy shop's awning and huddled against the shop's front wall, watching a sparse forest of legs and feet variously trudge, trot and traipse by. He closed his eyes, listening to the cadence of the footsteps, and melted happily against the rendered bricks. Oh, the noise of other people! Not ferrets, to be sure, so there was still room for improvement, but still: people! People who weren't Mercury or Deviran or Tundra or Sparky, or the handful of castle guard and keep staff who kept the place in order, or Chiara and her pegasus Jetstar who sometimes came to visit, or... Okay, fine, so he'd seen a *few* people the last few weeks, fine.

Still.

This lovely sea of anonymity and variation was welcome. Scents drifted over him, floral perfume and dog turds on someone's shoe, shoe-leather and sweat and a buttery croissant.

A fly buzzed past, tickling his ear.

Bystar flicked the ear, wrinkled his nose, decided he'd had enough people listening-slash-smelling for one day (especially given his allotted hour had to be close to over if he counted the return journey, which, maybe he would just conveniently forget about that and tell Mercury he'd assumed she meant an actual hour of *freedom*, travel-not-included), and headed into the shop, because he only had an hour and what else was he going to do.

Cool darkness was his first impression, then secondly a sneeze as incense, smoky and sweet, hit his nostrils. Rocks glittered and glimmered in all colours of the Eye (which was to say, all colours of the rainbow), wands of wood that smelled bittersweet and earthy or fruity and fresh or any manner of scents in between lay in wooden display boxes on glass shelves of all heights, and high up in the exposed rafters, drifts of dried herbs gathered. Bystar's nostrils twitched. Sage, for sure. A bunch of other things, but the scents were all swirling and mixing together, a dusty haze of... of enrichment.

Bystar sighed happily and threw himself on the polished wooden floor, writhing and wriggling in contentment.

"Hello there." The woman peering down at him with dark, sparkling eyes brushed at the lock of white hair escaping from her patterned red hairscarf and smiled, an ageless, creaseless face that seemed to radiate warmth. "Can I help you, or are you just looking?"

A hint of a frown drifted through Bystar's back mind: *Where are you?*

He brushed Mercury's voice aside. "Just looking," he said, "though if you like petting soft, friendly animals, I know someone in need of a belly rub." He shimmied, his back sliding on the polished floor.

The woman laughed. She did, however, stoop down obligingly to pat his stomach.

Bystar closed his eyes and lifted his chin, melting into the floor. Mmm. Enrichment felt as good as it smelled.

Yes, yes, okay, Mercury rubbed his belly for him sometimes, but did she smell—he inhaled deeply —like sage and roses while she did it? No. No she did not.

He batted away the thought that perhaps honeysuckle was, actually, just as nice as roses.

"A familiar, yes?" the woman said, scratching him under the chin.

He made a wordless noise, somewhere between pleasure and agreement.

"A familiar without his attendant, if I'm not mistaken."

Bystar tensed. Something in her tone... He narrowed his eyes at the glimmer in hers. "Yes," he said slowly. "I'm... on an enrichment break."

Should he have said that? Who knew. Either way, it was done now.

And he was done, ready to be on his way, off discovering more exciting things to tide him over for, presumably, the next month cooped up in that abominable, sunless room with Mercury.

He flipped over onto his feet.

"Oh, no," the woman silked. "I don't think you can possibly be going so soon. You see, I lost my cat recently, a dear old boy, Benji was his name, black as you like and so very soft, and since he's been gone I've been rather..."—she scooped Bystar up and it was too late to struggle—"...lonely."

She carried him to the wooden counter where a cash register skulked amid piles and clusters of glittering stones, small twigs, miniature bundles of herbs, boxes with brightly painted designs curling over them in a way that made Bystar's head hurt.

"Enrichment," the woman murmured as she placed Bystar down on the pile of tissue paper that covered the main surface of the counter. "Well, stay with me and you won't need to worry about *that.*"

Stay? No, Bystar couldn't stay, he had to go, he had... somewhere to be. Somewhere? Something? What was it he'd been doing again?

He sneezed.

"Aw, there now. Drink this, it will help."

Help? Help with what?

Help? Bystar, are you in trouble?

A pleasantly warm, lemony liquid appeared in front of Bystar's mouth. He sipped obediently, because although he thought there was probably a good reason not to, he couldn't quite grasp it right now.

"There," said the woman soothingly. "That feels better, doesn't it?" She ran a comforting hand down the length of his spine.

Bystar shivered.

"Mind the tissue paper, please."

Oh, yes, he'd curled his claws up and the lavender-soft paper was scrunching. Bystar tiptoed to the side, trying to make space for his long body between the stack of paper and the cottagey cluster of boxes and dried plants and trinkets.

"I'll bring you out back," the woman said. "You can play and enjoy some nice… enrichment. Okay?"

The front door to the shop rattled as its lock slid into place, the bell shivering goldenly.

Play. Play was good. Play was… was what he was here for, right?

Bystar rubbed his face against her hand as she scooped him up and swayed with him out to the back room.

The scents out here were a little less intense, a little less tangled—perhaps, if he'd been thinking clearly, Bystar would have noted: a little less *for show*. The lighting was brighter, more clean neutrals and less black, though where the light was coming from precisely Bystar couldn't tell; certainly there were no bulbs in the roof.

"Here," the woman said, balancing him atop the most intricate beige cat tree Bystar had ever seen, taller than the woman's shoulder, full of ramps and tunnels, platforms and climbing pegs and struts.

He wobbled slightly, the sweet, ricey scent of the cat who'd inhabited this tree wrinkling his nose. He stepped forward, blinking rapidly, dazed, disoriented—and the platform suddenly abandoned him, and his front paws were balanced on nothing—actually they were *un*balanced, unbalanced on nothing and his back feet couldn't hold him and he was falling...

Splat.

Ow.

Bystar lay still for a moment, cataloguing his hurts. Tail, probably dislocated. Left rear paw, ow. Right front leg, also ouch. Spine, probably mangled beyond repair and maybe he'd never walk again. He let himself flop limply to the ground, or the bottom of the cat tree, whatever it was.

Actually whatever-it-was was kind of scratchy, pleasant, mmm... He rubbed his back gleefully against it.

The woman chuckled.

Bystar shot her a glare, flipped himself over onto his feet, and licked his nose.

"Not as sure-footed as my old Benji, are you."

His glare deepened into a scowl. "'M not a *cat*."

She laughed.

Still. The cat tree now towering over him, with its intricate runways and maze of platforms and lovely scratchy covering... Mmm. Maybe he'd peti-tion Mercury for one of these. *Then* he'd feel nice and enriched.

A screech sounded from the back of the back room, ear-splitting, hair-curdling.

Bystar stiffened. "What was that?"

The woman grinned toothily. "*Fun.*"

Bystar gulped. Fun. Fun was... fun. He was here for... fun.

He shoved thoughts of the warm, cosy crevasse between the softness of the armchair and Mer-cury's curled legs aside.

"What... kind of fun?"

The woman opened her mouth, a red tunnel of doom—and something shook the cat tree above him like an earthquake.

Bystar backed away, a whimper escaping despite his best efforts.

Something monstrous and blue rose up over the cat tree, huge eyes glowing gold in the muted light.

It yowled.

Bystar ran.

He sprinted across the wooden floor, claws scrabbling for traction, the great blue *thing* hot on his heels.

No, a corner! *Can't get pinned in.*

He whirled, darted left, feinted right.

The thing, undeterred, bounded after him, hot breath ruffling the fur on Bystar's back as he skid-ded back toward the cat tree.

Upward he leapt, up and up and up, platform to platform, a sure-footed landing here, a scrabble for purchase there, all four feet planted firmly, now his left side dangling in mid-air as he tore up one of the ramps in the maze-like construction. *Enough enrichment!* he shrieked in the privacy of his own mind. *Enough enrichment!*

Air. Only air above him, and the blue thing that had somehow shrunk down to fit the cat tree was billowing out behind him, blue and snarling.

Bystar leapt, trusting to luck.

Better than devourment...

Midair, something hit him.

He sneezed, a great, hefty thing that tore through him, whirling him around in the air, and behind him was the ground, only he could rotate his head and there, there was the wooden floor, and if he rotated his body *just so*...

He flung his limbs out to slow the spin. Tucked a hind leg in a little to course correct.

Angled. Leaned...

And landed, limbs bowing as they absorbed the impact.

He shook all over, sat down to catch his breath, watched as his black paws shivered on the floorboards.

Wait.

Black.

Was the thing still following him?

He cast wildly around... But there was only the tall cat tree, and the woman, leaning against the bench, laughing silently with one hand pressed over her mouth and the other holding down her red hairscarf.

Bystar let go of just a little of the tension.

Which drew his attention to his feet again.

His black feet.

He wriggled his toes.

Yes. Definitely his feet. Definitely black.

Suspicion knotted in his chest. He pivoted to the woman—and his legs felt strange, long, and his tail was whippier than usual, and his fur, which had been tan with chocolate points, longish, stiff and wiry, was now short, sleek...

He narrowed his eyes at the woman. "What did you do?"

That was what he meant to say, anyway. Instead, what came out was, "Mau meooOOWWW!"

He froze.

I'm a...

I'm a...

The woman lowered her hands, lips still twitching mirthfully. "I did say you weren't as light on your feet as my old Benji. You shouldn't have flung yourself from the top like that, dear." She bent to run a hand over his sleek head, down his spine, running his tail through her fingers loosely. "It was the only way I could stop you from breaking your neck."

IS IT PERMANENT? came out as, "Rauw reeow MAU."

Is what permanent? Bystar, what have you done?

Mercury's suspicion-laded thought had him wincing. In all the excitement, he'd let that shield on his thoughts down again.

The woman scritched behind his ears.

Bystar leaned into it, enjoying—then jolted upright. *What am I doing?* He hissed, swatting at the woman's hand.

She laughed. "What?" she protested. "You can't tell me this isn't an *enriching* experience. And Bluey wasn't going to hurt you, he's just used to playing with Benji. Over-excited, I think," she said, glancing to the back of the room, behind the cat tree, where a faint blue glow cast up against the stone-pale wall. She ruffled Bystar's ears again. "I can understand that. We all miss Benji."

Bystar backed away—and away, and away, until—thump—his rear end hit the wall.

Mercury? he thought plaintively. She was never going to let him live this down, but mocking was better—probably, marginally, perhaps—than spending the rest of his life as a *cat. Mercury, I think...* He thought hard about a cat, sleek and black and with eyes that looked exactly like his own.

Uproarious laughter echoed in the halls of his subconscious. *Bystar,* don't *tell me you ran into Purrenya. Oh, Fate. I should let you out more often.*

He scowled.

At Mercury, at the woman, at the blue glow hunkering down in the far corner of the room.

Bystar spat at the lot of them.

Turned tail, and stalked elegantly out through the shop.

The woman's laughter followed him.

HE'D CAUGHT ANOTHER CARRIAGE EASILY ENOUGH—CATS could leap a lot higher than ferrets, it transpired—and hadn't been nearly as rattled to death by the time he'd made it back to the carriage stand nearest the castle.

Cats had longer legs, too, so the jog back home down the gravel path had been faster.

The breeze still sighed through the river red gums, wafting eucalyptus scent through the warm spring day. In the middle distance, a brown rabbit sat up to watch him pass.

Heh. Rabbits.

Next time he wanted enrichment, he'd content himself with chasing down the rabbits he often watched nibbling their way through the castle grass as he pressed his nose up against the cold glass.

Mind you, rabbit warrens, with all their twists and turns... He shuddered. A bit too much like the cat tree.

By the time he made it back to their tiny, cosy room, full of soft bedding and warm rugs, a thick glass window to keep out anything that wanted to chase him and a lap for him to snuggle into, Bystar would have gladly called the whole thing an *experience* and ignored it—if only for the fact that his feet were still black, his sides still sleek, and his voice still horribly feline.

Can you turn me back? he asked Mercury, eyes wide and mournful.

She snickered, and a tiny fireball flashed past his ear.

He ducked.

"I don't know," she said, smelling of honeysuckle and delight. "Your reflexes are faster as a cat."

He scowled, slashing at her with razor-sharp claws.

She laughed. "Alright, alright! I'll see what I can do. It might take a couple of days, though, to track down everything we need." A wicked grin, her eyes lit up; she reached down to pick him up, cradled him in her lap, rubbing his belly. "I do hope you'll find the experience *enriching* while you wait."

Bystar yowled, reached out to slash at the hand that was rubbing his belly...

...And stopped.

Because it was Mercury, and at least she was petting him, and who knew: maybe, with a few days as a cat, he could wriggle his way all the way to the top of Deviran's special bookcase, see if he couldn't shove a few books off the edge and cause some mayhem.

Now *that* would be enriching.

Bystar curled himself up in the velveteen crevasse between Mercury's lap and the side of the armchair—and purred.

Had Kafka Been
A Teenaged Girl

IT WAS FOUR O'CLOCK IN THE AFTERNOON WHEN STELLA woke up as a ladybird. The sun was glistening on the windowsill like a golden promise and the air smelled fresh and crisp, green with the surge of spring.

It wouldn't have been so bad if she'd been a normal-sized ladybird. That might have even been pleasant, for she could have spread her wings and flown through the narrow, open crack under the sash of the double-hung window, following the golden-green promises out to the yard where sweet white roses bobbed like bonneted maids in the gentle breeze.

She could have sailed along air currents gaily, drifting her way on tides of growth to the conifers beyond the lawn, and when she tired—having traversed so great a distance as to wear a little ladybird quite out—she could have alighted on the green-grey needles, their scent sharp and fresh, and found a tiny conifer cone to crawl into and take another nap.

Did ladybirds even like conifers? She didn't know.

In fact, Stella didn't know much right now, least of all why she had suddenly awoken from her slumber to find herself quite transformed—and, indeed, transfixed, for she could see herself in the mirror above her antique white dresser, and what she saw was enough to transfix anyone: a giant lady-bird, red and protuberant in the sunshine-white sheets of her bed, still dressed in her fine, lacy nightgown with her head upon the pillow and her feet amid the air.

The head—*her* head—was the strangest part, set against her body as was proper for a ladybird, but having a prominent, chitinous nose, all the more disconcerting for the similarity to its original shape; and the same with her eyes, still their regular shade of summer blue, but now set, staring, in a polished, black, chitinous face.

Worst, though, was the hair: long locks of raven or midnight—or, in fact, ladybird black—flowed from her ladybird face, cascading over her pillow like someone had stripped it off her while she slept and given a giant bug a wig.

A bug in a wig. That's what she was. A bug in a wig and a lacy nightgown, in her bed, at four-oh-three in the afternoon, according to the glaringly red numbers of her alarm clock.

All she'd wanted was some sleep.

Getting up, as it transpired, was an effort—as one could imagine it might be, if one were to imagine a giant ladybird lying on its back, six delicate feet waving ineffectually in the air, tangled in cobwebby folds of lace.

But eventually, Stella managed it, and felt such a great sense of relief that for a brief moment she forgot that she was now, apparently, an insect, and smiled.

The effect in the mirror was disconcerting to say the least, so she stopped.

She was contemplating the jump down off the bed when the door to her room burst open.

"Stella!" her brother shouted—and then he stopped, because really, what else could one expect him to do when faced with a giant bug in the bed where he'd expected to find his sister?

The fact that said bug still possessed the face and hair of said sister, although several shades darker, did nothing to allay his suspicions, and he ran into the room screaming, brandishing a bat.

It was not, fortunately for Stella, a baseball bat, or indeed any kind of bat used for sport—unless that sport was something akin to falconry, wherein one sets out with a leather-winged creature dangling from one's arm, and sets it loose to capture insects and other small prey, which actually sounds like rather a lot of fun.

But in any case, that would have requisited a live bat, and the one currently being flailed about by Owen, Stella's brother, was not alive—though, being made of polyester stuffing and synthetic minky fibres, it was not precisely *dead*, either.

What possessed him to brandish a stuffed bat at the giant ladybird currently residing in place of his sister, we shall never know, for as he approached the bed, he tripped upon the folders of homework Stella had left wantonly slung about on the floor earlier that day, and knocked his head against the corner of the bed.

Which left Stella with a problem—or, shall we say, an additional problem, because clearly awaking in the guise of a ladybird is problem enough for anyone.

Poor Owen's sudden loss of consciousness, however, seemed to Stella to be the more imminently pressing problem—she *was* a decent human being at heart, despite whatever her outward appearance may have currently suggested—and so she moved toward the door to call for help, ladybird hands, such as they are, being singularly unhelpful for things such as checking the pulse on a smallish human boy.

However, at this she encountered yet another problem, or An Additional Problem In Two Acts, because firstly, when she opened her mouth, only a strange sort of chirping issued forth, and secondly, she was too big to fit through the door, and ladybird bodies, being rather exoskeletal, did not appear to be malleable, no matter how hard Stella tried.

Realising abruptly that she looked very much like the excessively stupid fly that had been banging out its meagre brains against the glass of her window not two hours earlier, Stella stopped.

Right, she told herself. Pause for a moment, and take stock. Panic never got you anywhere. Except maybe into the body of a ladybird.

One: Am ladybird.

Two: Am wearing lacy nightgown. (How nightgown seems to have grown to accommodate new shape, will likely never know.)

Three: Unconscious child.

Four: Cannot get through door, cannot make noise to attract people.

Ah, she realised. There was the key. Perhaps she could not *call* for assistance, but she could certainly bash about and cause a ruckus, and perhaps if she was lucky, someone would attend.

She glanced about the room. Drawers and doors were all very well for making noise, but only if one was blessed with opposable thumbs. Ditto pulling books off her shelf.

No, the best she could see was the wooden slat blinds, at present a very appealing shade of honey brown in the late afternoon light.

Late, urgh. She was supposed to meet Tiffany at four-thirty for tennis.

Momentarily uncertain as to whether she was more dismayed by her brother's continued lack of consciousness or the apparent implausibility of making it to tennis on time, Stella buzzed toward the window and proceeded to raise a rather successful ruckus against the slat blinds.

Her father came running, only to raise his own ruckus as he entered the room and saw his son on the floor, possibly dead and apparently attacked by a giant, buzzing ladybird with a face rather like his daughter's.

Stella supposed she couldn't blame him. Screaming for her mother to phone a priest was maybe a little much, though.

Not that she *did* blame him. She'd have done the same.

But all the same, it hurt.

Though not as much as it did when he picked up one of her shoes—a high-heeled glittery sandal—and threw at it Stella with remarkably good aim, hitting her squarely on the... shoulder?

Stella supposed she didn't have shoulders anymore, really. But for want of a better word, that's what she was going to call it, and no one—least of all her shoe-wielding homicidal maniac of a father—was going to tell her different.

"Stop!" she shouted—or tried to. It came out as a kind of frantic chittering—which was probably a fairer indication of how she was feeling.

It occurred to her that he was unlikely to stop anything, given the situation now before him, and so, she decided, the most helpful thing she could do was to stop for him.

She hunkered down on her bed as quietly as she could, aiming for 'invisible' and hoping at least therefore to hit 'inconspicuous'.

No, that was ridiculous, a bright red bug in a lacy nightgown and wig the size combined of an excessively large Rottweiler was never going to be inconspicuous.

She did, however, at least seem to be hitting 'non-threatening', as indicated by the lull in her father's screaming.

Shooting several furtive looks in her direction, he edged into the room toward his son. Conveniently, right as he was reaching for Owen's neck—presumably that hunt for a pulse that had been Stella's first, unactionable, response—Owen opened his eyes and groaned.

Dad virtually had a heart attack, and Stella herself, having been engrossed with watching her father's hand reach closer, closer, closer to Owen's neck, all while his eyes darted toward her as though expecting her to leap from the bed at any moment and do to him whatever it was she'd apparently done to Owen, her whole body—it still counted as a body, she could call it a body, right?—tense with expectancy... Well. She may or may not have jumped a little at the sound issuing from Owen's mouth.

"Owen!" Dad was busy exclaiming, which at least had the side benefit that he was no longer glancing at Stella like she might attack him. "Are you okay? What happened? No, don't move," he added quickly as Owen struggled to sit. "Did the... Did it hurt you?"

No, though Stella grumpily, wishing she had arms that would accommodate a suitably huffy fold across her chest. *Though don't think the irony doesn't escape me.*

She'd threatened just yesterday that if he entered her room again without permission *one more time*, she'd kill him. Or, you know, maim him. Probably verbally assault him, actually, was what she'd meant. Anyway, it hadn't escaped her attention that he had entered her room without her permission yet again—though to be fair giant beetles hadn't been in the purvey of the original ban-from-bedroom—and that she had-but-hadn't been the one to injure him.

"No," Owen admitted generously. "I just slipped on all Stella's bloody crap here on the floor."

It was a mark of the irregularity of the situation that Dad did not comment on Owen-aged-nine's choice of language. "It didn't hurt you, then?"

Now now, Dad, no need to sound so surprised. Stella sniffed her irritation—and forgot the effect that that might have as air puffed not out her nose, but her sides. She jumped, tried to look at her own sides, remembered the general implications of having an exoskeleton, and by the time she'd stopped impersonating a small ratty terrier circularly defining a space for a nap, she could feel the eyes of her combined family members upon her.

Slowly, she turned back to face them.

"It doesn't look very dangerous, does it," said Dad, doubtfully.

Heh, just wait till I'm really *angry*, Stella thought.

At that moment, of course, two more joined the crowd of Stella's one-person—one-bug?—circus: it was Mum, in a flour-battered apron, and Tiffany, whose chestnut ponytail seemed, if anything, to have grown even *more* in height and volume since Stella had seen her this morning. But was anyone going to comment on *that*, the real miracle of the day? No. Instead, they were all going to hang out by the door, staring wide-eyed at her, who was merely a bug in a wig and a dress.

Stella sighed.

Air puffed out from her sides again and she tensed, but at least this time didn't jump.

"Stella," Mum said, because trust her to be the practical one, "why are you a ladybird?"

"And why are you wearing your nightie?" Tiffany said, punctuating her question with a loud crack of gum.

Stella couldn't speak, couldn't effectively mime, and couldn't even enact a very heartfelt headdesk —headbed—to express how she felt.

She flopped onto the bed, splaying her legs out on either side. No tennis. No catching up with Tiffany and the girls about all the salacious gossip that had occurred since Stella had gone home from school at lunchtime. No...

Well, that was fundamentally the point, wasn't it? No communication.

Something tickled Stella's for-want-of-any-more-appropriate-term face.

"Aw," said Tiffany, entering the room, stepping delicately over the still-sprawled Owen. "There now Stell, don't cry." She plucked a tissue from the box by Stella's bed and patted it gently on Stella's face.

Oh. Oh, crying, was that what that had been.

And... Oh. Niceness. That's what this was.

And, oh dear, that made her cry even more, and before she knew it, not only was she an awkward, exoskeletalled bug, she was an undignified *sobbing* exoskeletalled bug, and what that looked like she didn't even want to know.

"Do you know how this happened?" Mum asked, perching on Stella's other side.

Inhale (awkwardly, through her sides). No, but how to convey?

She tried shaking her head, which was so firmly attached to her body—at least she'd never forget it now, ha!—that the movement ended up as a whole-body shimmy that nearly knocked Tiffany and Mum from the bed.

Tiffany squeaked politely. Mum just lifted her arms in the air, holding herself clear until the Stella-quake subsided.

"No?" Mum said. "Okay then. Steve, go fetch her a glass of water, will you?"

Dad exited, shoulders rounded in a slightly sheepish manner, dragging the now-recovered Owen along with him.

"Don't worry, Stella dear. We'll make this work."

"I'll bring my notes by every day from school," Tiffany added. "Though I imagine tennis will be a bit of a bummer now without you."

Deep down in Stella's little bug heart—or whatever it was she had that passed for one right now—a conflict was occurring. On the one hand—did she have any hands? Were any of them hands? Was it like octopuses and one pair were arms-with-hands, and the rest legs-with-feet? Or, well...

Wings. She buzzed a little, experimentally, and yes, sure enough, she had those, so—on the one *wing* she was infinitely grateful that there was some response to be had to seeing her that didn't involve a) unconsciousness, b) throwing sandals, c) shouting, or d) all of the above.

On the other... wing...

Well, Mum and Tiffany were acting as though they expected this to be *permanent* now, weren't they? And that thought was... well...

Depressing.

Stella went still on the bed, letting whatever platitudes it was that Mum and Tiffany were speaking wash over her like white noise, like rain, like the wind gently teasing through the branches of the conifers outside.

Communication.

It all came down to communication.

(Another momentary irony, of course, since she was presently doing her level best to ignore everything that was being said.)

Communication, communication, communication.

That was the key to it all.

Something niggled in the back of her brain. (Brain? Yes, ladybirds definitely still had brains, that was good.)

She dove from the bed.

Mum and Tiffany squeaked as she plunged past them to the floor.

But somewhere here, in this mess of schoolwork and books, somewhere...

Rifling through paperwork was significantly more challenging when your feet not only lacked opposition in their digits, but were also covered in tiny hairs designed to *stick*—and when you could smell literally everything they touched.

She hadn't noticed it so vibrantly before, because she'd primarily been either a) on her own bed, or b) trying not to let her brother accidentally expire. But now, the sensory assault coming from her feet (why on *earth* was there not only a nose, but an exceptionally *prominent* one, *right* in the middle of her face if it wasn't going to perform *any* of the usual nasal functions?) was overwhelming: paper, yes, but plastic and the smell of pencil graphite and the bitter taste of ink and her own stinky handprints and a smear of something that smelled like rotten banana...

Humans. Absolutely disgusting.

She froze, rigid for an instant as she wondered

briefly about the more *biological* aspects of being a ladybeetle.

Oh well. She'd conquer that when it came to it.

Mum and Tiffany had joined her on the floor, kneeling at her sides again and doing their best to help her shuffle through the assorted exercise books and paperwork, which was admittedly much easier because they could hold things up to her face, whereas she had to do the awkward shuffle of a scavenging chicken: scratch scratch with the feet, then step back to peer at the mess and see if anything interesting had resolved.

For a heart-jolting moment, Stella thought she'd forgotten how to read. Then she realised that the book Mum was presently holding in front of her face was simply the for-lols-and-funsies notebook she'd been keeping with The Girls as they absolutely did not pass notes back and forth in class under the guise of sharing explanatory lesson notes, and the cover was written in code.

Her pulse (*dammit* she was going to have to take an anatomy class on beetles) settled back to something more regular, and she did the whole-body shake in the negatory. No. Not that book.

"Oh, hold on, I know which one she wants," Tiffany said, her ponytail practically vibrating with purpose. She furrowed through the paperwork, wafting the scent of bubblegum and cheap floral perfume pretending to be expensive toward Stella's... Okay Stella had no idea what to call the organs on her sides that were now apparently the stand-ins for her nose, but whatever the heck they were, they were smelling Tiffany quite overwhelmingly.

"Here," Tiffany said, holding up Stella's history textbook.

Stella whole-body nodded.

"Right, perfect," Tiffany said. "Now, this isn't going to be fast, and I imagine, Stell, it's going to be pretty frustrating for a while, but stick with it, okay? We're in this together."

Mum's brow furrowed. "I feel like that's the thing I should have said."

Tiffany flicked her a glance—"Probably."—and flicked open the history book to the double-page spread on Morse code.

Stella couldn't help it: she bounced up and down just a little.

Tiffany tore the two pages from the book— Mum flinched; "Urgh, Tiffany, that's a ninety dollar textbook"—snatched some tape out of Stella's school pencil case, and taped the Morse code up on Stella's mirror. "There," she said, surveying her work with her hands on her hips. "Actually, hang on..." She peeled the tape slowly off the mirror and repositioned the pages lower down, closer to Stella's current eye height. "*There.*"

Stella stared at the code. Shuffled a little closer to the mirror. Stared some more. Slowly, laboriously, and with sheer unbridled *boredom* at how long the process took tapped out the letters T-H-A-N-K-S.

Well. This was communication at its least efficient.

"Aw. No worries." Tiffany leaned in for the world's most awkward, one-sided hug.

Not that Stella didn't want to contribute a side. Just that, you know. Having exoskeletal sides made sharing a side more difficult.

Okay, okay: so it was inefficient but inefficient wasn't the same as ineffective. Mum swiped a tear away from her face, Dad returned—showing some forethought—with a shallow bowl full of water, which he edged in, tense and pale-faced, to place on the ground before his daughter-apparent where she stood at the mirror, and Stella was definitely, absolutely, positively *not* going to cry again.

"I always knew you were cockroach at heart," Owen said affectionately.

Stella sniffed—and didn't jump, or even tense this time at the puff of air from her sides—and wondered if it would take too long to spell out I-D-I-O-T-,-A-F-F—the Aff standing for (affectionate).

"What are we going to do about school?" Dad said, just shy of wringing his hands in the doorway.

Mum shrugged. "We pay a fortune. They always go on about how good they are at accommodating student needs. Let them accommodate this. And if you hate it," she added to Stella, "I'll homeschool you."

Stella shuddered. Mum shuddered. The house probably shuddered at the thought of the two of them trying to be civil all day.

But Stella appreciated it nonetheless.

T-Y, she tapped out. Thank God for standard texting abbreviations.

"Look, my primary concerns," said Tiffany, leaning back with her elbows against the wall and cracking her gum again, "are exactly how much Esther-Louise is going to *crack* her *nut* when I tell her what happened, and whether or not Stella can carry me on her back." She grinned, the cracked grin she always gave when Stella was upset over something not at all trivial but also utterly out of their hands.

It was a measure of their relationship both that Tiffany had a specific grin for such an occasion, and that Stella knew it.

Stella couldn't grin back, couldn't make any sort of expression with human familiarity—oh, wait, she did have her regular eyes now, didn't she.

She gave her best Duchenne, hoping Tiffany would get the point.

Tiffany wrinkled up her face, pleased, and patted Stella on the shoulder-approximate. She had, apparently, gotten the point.

"Well then," said Mum. "What a to-do. I suppose I'll go call the school, book an appointment with the principal, all that."

"And I'll..." said Dad, casting around the room for something useful to do. He practically lit up as he spotted the mess of books. "I'll clean up Stella's room. See..." He swallowed. "I'll, uh, chat to you about what I can do to make it more comfortable for you, okay Stell?"

On the one wing, his bright discomfort scoured against Stella's sense of pride. On the other, his bashful, red-cheeked attempts to be helpful were, well, really rather sweet.

Stella Duchenned in his direction.

His mouth wrinkled up, bunching to one side in something that probably once somewhere in a past life was a smile.

Stella took it.

In the doorway, Owen hugged his stuffed bat to his chest. "My sister," he breathed, eyes wide in awe, "is a bug. This is the *best* thing *ever*. Mu-um!" he shouted as he bolted away. "Can I go to Michael's? I have to tell him about Stella!"

Stella shuffled meekly to the side as Dad set to work clearing up the books.

Tiffany patted her fondly again. "Geez," she said. "All it took to get perfectly smooth skin was turning into a bug, hey. I told you you were taking your skincare regime too seriously."

Stella chuckled. Not, like, externally, because that would no doubt have been horrifying. But, you know: internally.

Okay. Okay so perhaps this wasn't going to be that much worse than being a life-sized ladybug wafting out over the white bonnet roses into the conifers to nap in a cone after all. *Perhaps* it was entirely possible to live a full—she caught sight of herself in the mirror again—*well-rounded* (ha ha) life like this after all.

Not without its challenges, of course.

But no life ever was.

Stella settled down to the lengthy task of spelling out her current most-pressing request: P-L-E-A-S-E G-E-T T-H-I-S S-T-U-P-I-D N-I-G-H-T-I-E O-F-F M-E.

A Plague On Both Your Colonies

Once, I had no word for 'dark'. The whole wide world was dark, from end to end, and so there was no need to name it. And, when all is said and done, what's in a name? We have no need to name that which is all-encompassing, not when there is no supposition or even imagining of any other option.

I am me and you are you; there is sour and there is sweet; my colony is mine and the not-my colonies are other. These things bear natural contrasts, edges that demand language to define them.

But when there is only dark—has only ever been dark—why define it?

Nevertheless, once, there was light, blinding, brilliant, awesome, and I, like all my colony—like all the colonies—shrank away in fear as it passed first from the beginning of the world, called east, to the end, called west, then back again.

So now, it is with confidence that I may say to you: the world is dark.

In all my life, I have never been more grateful for comparison. How else would I know to say that Jillian is as brilliant as the light that rises in the east, from whence comes all our sustenance?

Jillian is fair as the sugars that sustain us, sweet as starch, and her image is to me like the great Pulsing of the universe that surrounds us continually, the great rhythm of life we hear but cannot touch.

Would that I could touch her.

Alas, in all this sour world there is but the trace of her to comfort me, for she is Lac, and I am of the Pep, separated by the tides of enmity that flow between us.

It is as I am lingering over an old chem trail of hers, left many feasts ago, that I am jostled by an unfamiliar individual. Her taste, however, is not entirely strange: this is a member of the Lac, same as my Jillian.

I tense, uncertain, and poise myself to slide away.

Friend, the stranger's chem trails announce. *I bring a message.*

Anticipation ripples through me at that. 'Message' could also mean a warning, I suppose, but were this individual here to warn me from my love forever, she would have stated that more clearly. *A message?* I repeat.

Jillain pines for want of thee, she chems to me.

I practically vibrate. *And I for her.*

A proposal, then, she chems. *Jillian will meet with thee near the northerly aspect of the end of the world, three feasts' hence from now.*

She is gone before I can reply, and although I could shout chem trails out at her retreat, and she would receive them, that would leave them exposed for anyone to stumble on until they dissipate; secrets are not thusly kept.

Three feasts hence.

I can school myself to patience for three more feasts, even though the first feast of this noisetime has passed already, and I will have to bide myself through sad hours that will seem long before the third feast hence arrives.

Still, many of those hours can be spent in travel, at least; it will take at least two feast times, maybe more, to make it to the end of the world.

IT IS SOMEWHERE NEAR THE MIDDLE OF THE QUIET WHEN A scuffle breaks out. From the intensity of the chem trails, I judge it to be somewhere back toward the scape I usually call home, a place I haven't been in many quiets.

The same number of quiets as those since Jillian and I first met, if one were keeping count.

Were I to go home, my split-father would sense immediately something was amiss; indeed, he likely already has, if Bun's not-so-subtle questioning about my health and wellbeing is anything to go by.

I care not.

Not about Bun's questions, not about my split-father and his concerns, and not about the scuffle now ensuing. 'Tis a story old to my senses as to my mind, and I am weary of it. Time and again we have been warned: put aside our differences and co-operate, or pay the price.

And there, in fact, again: as I slide determinedly away, toward the world's end, away from friend and foe alike, a chem trail strong enough to have taken almost all the energy of a feast reaches me from he who calls himself our Prince: another disturbance like this and lives will be paid forfeit, for the sake of peace.

I do not blame him for such a weighty repri-mand. Even now the ever-present crowd around me is restless and on edge, the bitter scent and taste of Helio thick around us, a reminder of the true price of our fighting: foolish, to fight among ourselves when a true enemy masses at our bor-ders, growing in both number and in strength while we whittle ourselves and those who ought to be our allies down to naught.

Rumours say the world will end if we cannot put away our hate.

Rumours—some say prophecies—of a sour-ness so strong we cannot withstand it, of a burning pit carved into the very surface of the world, of groaning and straining as the whole universe is brought low and the plague of Helio runs rampant.

I should care about such things.

I don't.

SHE IS THERE.

I sense her well before we are close enough to communicate safely, not any specific chem trail laid for deliberate communication, but the general scent and taste of her passage, a pleasant sourness more mellow and less sharp than the world in which we live, distinct from the sweet smell-taste of the Strep clan who live here.

I am also aware of the end of the world, hovering there just out of reach, waiting to suck me away with all the souls of the deceased.

Sometime, I too will expire, and my soul will dissipate into the sourness of our surrounds, and I will be passed from this world into whatever may come next. Now is not that time.

I reach Jillian and gently press against her. She receives me warmly, and secretly we confer our blessings on each other so none may hear.

For how long will you love me? Jillian chems.

For as long as there is time, I reply. *I swear it on the feasts.*

Oh! Jillian's chem is vibrant, an expression of strong emotion. *Do not swear by the feasts, as inconstant and irregular as they are!*

Then what? I chem fervently, pressing firm against her. *Tell me by what I should swear.*

Nothing. Her chem is so faint I strain to sense it. *Or if you will, swear by yourself, and yourself alone.*

I will swear by that, as long as I do live, I whisper to her. And live therefore I must, which means never going home. This matters not; I have no care for feuds which are not mine.

Jillian presses against me, whispering sweet nothings, and I lose myself in her embrace.

RUMBLINGS REMIND US OF OURSELVES, AND HASTILY WE part—not far, but just so far as to remember where one of us begins and the other of us ends.

It is not the next feast yet, she chems lazily across the infinitesimal distance between us. *It cannot be.*

Oh, but love, I chem, *it is. You'll be missed.*

Never. She smooches up against me and I cave to her touch. *It is only some rumblings of the universe beyond. It is not feast time yet.*

It could be the rumblings of the universe. At times it does that.

But it is not. *You must return,* I chem as gently as I can. I detach myself from her embrace, unable to prevent the gentle sway of sorrow that leaks from me into our surroundings.

The Strep clan members who surround us ease away in response—whether to give privacy or to avoid the unpleasant emotion, I can't be sure.

Above us in the sour swirl of existence, the first-fruits of the feast arrive: molecules of bread, swirling, ephemeral scent-glimpses of hard cheese, something sweet and sharp.

It is the feast, Jillian chems across the wider distance between us, thick with the taste of her mourning. *I must go.*

I told you that, I think but do not chem.

Many things are best left unsaid, especially as the distance grows.

She vanishes between the Step, her comforting gentle sourness slowly erased by the sweet taste-scent of the Step themselves—and then, all at once, erased in a rush as the feast arrives in full, and for the next several hours, I busy myself consuming food.

The mango chutney is to die for.

I MUST GO SOMEWHERE, OF COURSE, EVEN IF I DO NOT WISH to go back home, and several feasts and a quiet or two later, I find myself nearer than I would have liked to the boundary between the colonies who have been part of this world since before time began, and those who have but newly arrived: the Helio.

They mass in growing numbers at our borders, and I clench with shock as I realise how large their colony has grown: a stench comes strongly from them, reminiscent of the rotten smells that, very rarely, drift back from the end of the world.

Perhaps the prophecies are right. If the Helio

stink like the end of the world, maybe they are its heralds.

I hurry home, because no matter what the Prince has said, it is still Jillian of whom I think: if the world ends truly, then she will too.

IT'S AT THE THRESHOLD OF PEP TERRITORY THAT HE appears, narrow and pinched and chem trails full of anger and of pugilism, masking the warm-sour smell that as a Lac he ought to have, like Jillian.

What are you doing here? I chem. Then, strongly, with all the energy I can muster, *Go away. I have greater things to deal with now than you.*

Oh yeah? he chems—a witty repartee. *Try me.*

I do not. I turn away, pushing through the crowds of mingled Staph and Pep here at the liminal edge of home.

Something sharp catches me.

Pulse surrounding, somehow, this ever-loving fool that Jillian is cursed to call her split-mate, has sharpened up a granule of sand that he wields now now at me.

Sand is rare, priceless, and this *buffoon*, this cultureless *monstrosity*, has somehow found the means to carve a weapon.

Would I had a more sufficient way to express exasperation than merely chemming it at him.

Remm, away!

I whirl my attention to Bun, who has appeared through the thinning crowd, presumably to question me for the sake of my split-father again—and I am reminded of my purpose here. *Bun,* I chem to him urgently, the taste of it heavy around us as I push the message past the nearest ring of Staph that constitute the ever-present crowd. *The Helio. We must do something.*

I'll do something, Bun chems as he draws close. *I'll eat him for threatening you like that.*

Please don't, I chem with a shudder, not only for the trouble it would bring but for the instant, immediate sensation that it conjures: Tybon, inside me, made part of me, consumed. *Blech.* I shudder my disgust again.

Oh, Tybon chems, the sand-weapon waving, *I disgust you do I. Well let me tell you, villain—*

What he intends to tell me I will forever wonder, for Bun leaps between us, right for the weapon—

He will fall upon it—

So I leap too, and knock him aside—

Only it's too late and the fall is wrong—

The sand-weapon clatters down.

I am bloated. Full.

A chem-shout streaks past, followed by another: from near and far, Lac and Pep are drawn to the scent of my conflict, and in they rush, with hunger for the fray.

I edge aside as chem trails rise around me, so thick it becomes hard to distinguish one from another.

Oh, Pulse. Oh, life-giving, ever-loving Pulse, I have consumed not only my enemy, but my friend; and the first not only my enemy, but Jillian's split-mate.

I expand in horror. What have I done?

I AM GRATEFUL FOR THE DARKNESS, I SUPPOSE. IMAGINE IF the world were always light. A shudder-worthy thought. To be exposed, so naked, and so seen...

I cannot face my Jillian after this.

I cannot face my split-father.

But with the Helio massing on our borders, I must. And so, steeling myself, reluctantly I enter my home territory.

The smell-taste of thoroughly digested feasts surrounds me, comforting and familiar. This, I imagine, is what the afterlife must smell like, if there is such a thing.

But halfway toward the place I expect to find my split-father, creeping dread surrounds me.

And then the Prince appears.

You. It is neither question nor command as he blocks my way with his bulk, his heavy, musty odour overriding all other communication. *You will be sent on to the afterlife.*

I shrink in desperation. *No*, I chem with wild desperation. *No, please. I must see my split-father first. I must warn him...*

But the Prince shoves me back the direction I have come. *One feast,* he chems. *You have have one final feast to make your reparations. If I taste you before then...*

I shudder. *Please tell my father of the Helio,* I chem. *They are massing. Their colony is growing. Their numbers will be unstoppable. The fighting, it must end. My father can stop it. He must.*

There is a long pause, in which the jostling of the crowd around us creates a quiet susurrus and the pulsing of the universe is heard: *Ba-boom. Ba-boom. Ba-boom.* The rush of the lifeblood that sustains us beneath the substance of the world, somewhere deep beyond.

I agree, Prince chems. *I would not have thought that you would.*

I do, I chem—a witty repartee—and fade away into the crowd.

It is Jillian's messenger, and she does not know what I have done.

Perhaps she approaches me a little differently, recognising some difference in my scent—an inevitable occurrence, regardless of what it is one feeds on—great Pulse of the universe preserve me, shame drips from me at the thought of what I have fed on since the last feast—but she does not know.

She cannot.

She would not chem me if she did.

Instead, she sidles up close to chem with privacy. *Trouble*, she chems, and I tense.

Perhaps she does know.

Jillian's split-mother, she continues, and I relax for just an instant before she continues: *She is sending Jillian to the Helio.*

What?! My chem is vibrant enough that the crowd around us surges away from the bitter taste of disgust.

Faint chems of disapproval swirl around us momentarily, dissipating with the gentle, rhythmic wafting of our sour surrounds.

Why? I chem more circumspectly, all too aware of the muttering around us.

She thinks to offer a sacrifice. To negotiate for peace.

In my mind, I sense the vastness of the Helio once more, the strength of their taste growing, blooming like a foul infection—which of course, is what they are.

I squinch down into a scowl. *It won't work.*

I know, the messenger chems back. *That's why I found you.*

I am heavy—with guilt, and physically, with the weight of my last horrific meal. *There's naught that I can do.*

Untrue. I know you. She trusts you. You can stop them.

You don't know me. That chem tastes like sour betrayal—my own betrayal, betrayal of Jillian.

She's trusting you, the messenger chems softly. *I know you'll do what's right.*

If the Prince tastes me again, or even crosses a chem trail I have left, he will speed me to my death.

Either way, I have only until the next feast. After that, he'll find me, will use every resource in his power to bring me down.

The world isn't big enough to hide from him for long.

Wait! I push the chem trail out past rows of semi-slumbering Pichia. *Wait. Okay. I'll come.*

THE ENTIRE WORLD IS RUMBLING BY THE TIME THE MESsenger draws to a halt, quakes trembling beneath us all. Our surrounds taste thick and cloying with terror, chems swirling back and forth as the message is spread: the Helio. The Helio are coming.

Sure enough, I can sense by the changes in the surrounds that the Helio are advancing, their foul taste-smell increasing, growing, burgeoning, slowly taking over—just as they are.

And underneath it all, an even sourer scent, a burning; and I am consumed with thoughts of a pit carved into the trembling surface of the world, and taste of agony, rumbling vibrations that I cannot tell if real or simply imagined... And the world, it's surely ending.

I am frozen.

I am quaking.

I am the world, and I am ending too.

A scream, a thin, drawn-out chem trail of desperation, swirling fleetingly past.

Abruptly, I am jolted into motion. It's Jillian.

I race along her chem trail, desperation of my own lending speed.

Chem trails flash back and forth as the crowd tries desperately to stand against the Helio.

The taste of dying souls fills the surrounds.

Hurriedly, I chant last rites for them as I go, on the chance that no one else is able. Too weighty to risk the alternative.

Jillian! I force the chem trail out from me with so much energy that I stumble. Pace it, I remind myself. No point reaching her if my energy is depleted when I get there.

Something whaps me, and again I stumble.

I told you if I found you you'd be dead, the Prince intones, no trace of emotion in his chem.

No! I chem back frantically. *No, not now, just wait! Jillian, I have to save her, I have to stop her split-mother!*

Would you could, the Prince intones again. *Would, oh Remm, you could.*

But I can, if you'll just let me reach her!

The Helio advance, so near now there is little else to taste.

Jillian!

The faintest of chems. Distress.

Jillian...

A burst of anger surges over us, driving back the foreguard of the Helio.

It is my split-father, and for an instant hope suffuses me. He is here! Help is at hand! He is driving back the Helio and Jillian's colony has arrived and perhaps, perhaps there is time, and I can save her...

His death shall not be vain! he chems. And my split-father overleaps me, and as I am once more frozen, stunned by the enormity of his passing, the energy in his chem trails so intense I too am driven back by them, I note with recognition another scent that swirls.

It is the messenger.

She chems last rites.

She chems last rites for Jillian.

Together! my split-father roars.

Together! Jillian's split-mother rages.

I keep my vows, the Prince intones. *I told your split-father you were dead, the penalty paid for sins as I decreed. I declared you dead; thus shall you be.*

Split-father thought me dead; is this rage he bears for me?

Then reality intrudes. It does not matter what he thought. In a moment, it will be truth. I hunker down, awash with bitter fear.

But no. Jillian has proceeded me. Jillian has gone on, has exited the world—or is exiting, her soul caught up amid the whirl and swirl of battle.

The Helio stumble back.

The Prince bears down on me.

I hold myself as upright as I can. I will not face him with the bitter taste of fear, but the sweet, sweet scent of hope.

Jillian's soul is but a little way above, staying for mine to keep her company.

The Prince lunges.

I burst. The sweet chemistry of hope permeates my immediate surrounds.

It is the end of the world—for me, if not the colony.

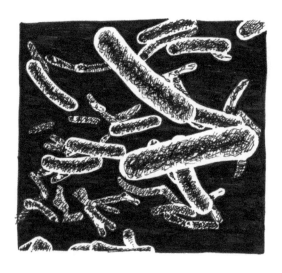

To Walk One Path Alone

I T'S HARD TO TELL DIRECTIONS IN THE REALM—WITH any precision, anyway. Sounds seem to come from all around whether they mean to or not, smells rise in enveloping miasmas that temporarily befuddle the senses before bursting like a cold shower in glittering light blue or yellow or green or other colours depending on which part of the Realm you're in.

This part of the Realm does its best to appear as a forest as often as it can, oaks and maples and suchlike for the most part, or things close enough so as to make little difference. The scents and sounds still float and change, though.

And so, as Saefda drifts along through her day (or whatever passes for a day in these parts; some-times that shifts too), casually brushing aside the scent of lemon pepper, a bubble of some kind of sharp, metallic zing, and a burst of juicy rainforest, she ignores the crying sound at first.

Her own footsteps drift through the leaf litter, a rustle and soft thud that seem to lift from the ground like a shadow given wings, each one flying along beside her like a little pet, or a flock of butterflies, or music. She brushes the vines back from the past—she used to come this way often, but she hasn't now, not for a couple of decades at least, and no one else has come this way either.

Why would they, when she never told anyone what she'd found out here? The only one who knows what lies at the end of this path is Jasmari, and although Saefda knows she would appreciate the gifts that Saefda could offer her from a visit to the end of the path, Jasmari hasn't called in her debt just yet.

So it doesn't matter, either way. There's no rush. The path is the path, or the path is not the path, or the path is *a* path but not *the* path, or else it's all just creeping vines with tiny white flowers that sometimes turn into butterflies that sting, hanging from things the humans would call oaks or maples, beeches or hickory—though of course, in truth, they're none of those, the trunks much taller, the leaves much thinner and shining faintly with iridescence that holds the full spectrum of the rainbow, even if it has a little more green than anything else.

Saefda approves of that. Green is the colour of her tunic and her eyes, the colour of the leaves' magic and the grass, the colour of things that grow —the colour of her Hall. Even though it's named the Hall of Wood.

On a deep, base level, that still irks her.

But now, her footsteps fluttering around her, the vines drifting lazily like sea kelp in tides, or else snapping taut at the touch of some tiny, living thing they can devour, scents rising and bursting and rolling and cresting—leaf litter, mushroom, orange sherbet and mangoes—the crying sound comes again, and although it rolls around her like thunder from above, Saefda cocks her head, because the sound, the crying, is probably actually coming from right ahead, just off the edge of the path.

She swims her way through the forest, slow, languid movements for her but to any watching eye not of the People—not that there are many of those in the Realms, not now, not *here*—a rapid, astonishing dance that sees her whirl her way past oak trunks wider than houses, under beech branches thicker than thighs, dancing through the long-fingered twigs of a maple like a green-glowing firefly, her long red hair flaring around her like autumn leaves falling. And she draws to the edge of the path, where the crying thing waits.

Saefda was *expecting* something of the People, of course, because not only is this the Realms, which tend to drive humans mad, and not only is this in the Hall of Wood, unfriendly to humans in the way of tall, secret growing things that have no regard for the hubris of constructed things, it's also—as aforenoted—one of the most remote corners thereof, where no one has been in years.

And yet—Saefda blinks, a long, slow gesture like an assessing cat—here is not only a something, not only a someone, but here is a *human*, in one of the remotest corners of the Realm that one could possibly imagine.

Well.

Saefda cocks a hip, folds her arms, purses her lips and scowls down at the tiny being currently bawling in emerald grass taller than it is.

Nearly human, anyway.

Will be human, give or take a few years.

Only, of course, it's a pre-speech baby in a remote corner of the Realm; it doesn't *have* a few years, neither under its belt, as it were, nor ahead of it. Changelings aren't known for their longevity this side of the dimensional divide.

Saefda draws her arms in more tightly, tasting bitterness in the back of her throat. Ugly, wretched thing, so helpless, so *stupid*. So unlike the People, the ones who are thought or called or believed into being, who arrive at the fringes of fae villages whole and fully formed, a complete identity ready for assimilation. Adult, if such a word could be applied to something that never had a childhood at all.

Such a more civilised way to do things than this repulsive mess that's barely more than a congealing of bodily fluids and instincts.

Deep in her heart, old, ossified memories prickle her with shards of bone.

She should be going. She has places to be that she hasn't been to in years, and the time is right, and the time is now, and the forest needs her.

The baby will die here alone, but what of it? There are billions—literally—of the stupid brats to take its place, and if it's found its way out here somehow, the mother will have already given up hope. No human returns from the Realms.

Somewhere in the forest, a bird-like creature chirps. It could be near, or far, or there could be several all around, such is the thrown-nature of its call here in the deep of wild, wild woods.

Saefda sighs.

Her debt to Jasmari can wait.

She picks up the child.

Cradles it against her shoulder.

Pats its bottom gently until the wailing ceases.

Then Saefda turns, and with infinitely more slowness than she made her way in, Saefda picks her way back out of the heart of the forest.

THE CHILD GROWS QUICKLY INTO A ROSY-CHEEKED TOD-dler, babbling sounds that are far too human as Saefda tries to teach her—it's a her, Saefda has decided—to warp her tongue around the language of the Wood Hall.

Saefda hasn't been back to the forest. Not yet. She will—she needs to—but time passes more slowly in the Realms. The People are in less of a hurry than the humans.

It's easy to be patient when the frailest of your people live a couple centuries, at worst.

It would be even easier, Saefda imagines, to be patient as one of the Old Folk; once, legend has it, they lived to be more than a thousand years apiece.

Saefda kicks a door shut in the kitchen, a willowy one that, when closed, looks of a piece with the cabinet surrounding it, just as the cabinet itself looks more like a natural growth on the inner side of a tree trunk than anything constructed.

Sometimes, things look exactly like what they are.

Across the room on the mat of moss, the child gurgles happily.

The child's life will be even shorter than Saefda's.

At the front door, which is in actual fact little more than a thinning in the willow treehouse's trunk where the People may pass freely through (or at least, those of the Wood Hall may), a presence announces itself, the doorway glowing green like night-glowing fungus.

Her life will be even shorter than those of her kind if another of the People find her here.

Saefda waves her hand.

Roots detach from the floor around the moss rug, turning the air over with a sweet, sappy scent, sweeping the child up and folding her back down into the floor itself.

Her cry of protest is cut off as the roots seal back over as though they'd never moved.

Saefda waves at the door, and the energy of the willow shifts, the sap shifting subtly in the phloem, the song subtly different as the enchantments that seal the house begin to lift, the taste of it thick in the air—just slightly sapward of pollen, sweet and green and complex.

In a moment, someone who looks even younger than Saefda materialises on the mossy welcome mat, bringing with her the smell of violets. 'Looks' younger is key: beautiful, dark-skinned Jasmari may be only a decade older than Saefda, but she never lets anyone forget it.

"Another dragon is loose," she announces without introduction.

Saefda sighs. This is Jasmari's personal vendetta, and she is often indifferent to others' disinterest in it. With any luck though it means she will be equally disinterested in the squeaking and squeals faintly audible below the floor; Saefda forces herself not to wince, not to show her hand.

"Have they allowed you leave to search for it?" Saefda enquires politely.

Jasmari remains stiff, taut, eyes flashing as her hands clench by her side. "My father," she spits, "still refuses."

Saefda's lips purse of their own accord. That is a matter between Jasmari and her family alone, that they will not allow her passage to the second world—the human world.

Saefda cannot blame them, really. Jasmari is too sympathetic to the humans as it is.

Guilt tugs at the corners of Saefda's heart as she remembers how Jasmari befriended her when no one else would, but she brushes that quickly aside. "Will you take refreshments?"

"No."

Good. The child is wearying of confinement.

Saefda cannot blame her. Her heart pounds. If Jasmari hears her...

"I will send my sprites to comfort you," Saefda says, a traditional parting line that varies from pat and meaningless, to a promise of actual, tangible aid. She's not sure right now how she means it; doesn't really care too much, so long as Jasmari gets the point.

Jasmari doesn't care too much either. "Just do your part," she says. "You owe me, and I'd have my debt repaid before sunset." She nods curtly and is gone.

Saefda waits to the count of forty-nine, her heart knocking crudely at her chest. She does indeed owe Jasmari, a debt of kindness given, and she'd intended to see that debt repaid.

She glances at the floor that hides the child. She'd intended to see that debt repaid. Soon. Soon enough. Once the child was safe.

Now it seems she has until sunset to make *sure* the child is safe, and partly that safety comes through clearing debts unpaid, for once the debt is called to account and a timeline given, the People are bound by laws no less immutable than human physics to accede.

If not...

Well. The monstrosity the humans call *hydrogen bomb* does not exactly *break* physics—fusion does sustain life, after all, though that's a path whose contemplation leads to madness—but no one wants to be at the centre of a detonation.

So.

The debt has been reclaimed and now Saefda has until sunset to repay it, unless she wishes to see her own equivalent of nuclear fusion that will end her just as surely—and just as suddenly.

A counterpoint to these thoughts, the metronome in her head reaches the count of forty-nine and Saefda waves her hand again. The roots in the floor of the willow-tree room lift once more and out comes the child, face smudged with sweet-scented dirt, one hand sticky with syrupy sap.

She sticks her fingers in her mouth. Giggles. Stares up at Saefda as drool seeps from her mouth around her fingers, making a thin paste with the remnants of the sap.

Disgusting.

Saefda fetches a cloth from the kitchen sink— nothing more than a rounded hollow in the smooth surface of the bench, all one with the willow, a place water appears when she needs it and disappears when she does not.

Tenderly, she prises the child's fingers from her mouth and dabs clean her face.

The child pats Saefda's face lovingly, if not gently. Traces of sap bleed into Saefda's lips. She licks them away with the tip of her tongue, the sweet lifeblood of the tree who provides her with a home.

Light gleams in the child's less clean hand, rose pink.

Saefda inhales sharply. "What is it you have there?"

She unfurls the child's sticky, sweaty fingers and the fragrance of apple blossoms fills the air. A gem, no bigger than the child's fingernail, lies in her sweaty palm. It is rose pink. It is cube cut. It is a gem Saefda had thought long lost.

She doesn't mean to snatch, but this is it, the Rosa Fraenqa, the thing the universe has been waiting for and the reason she hasn't made it to that place in the forest again before now.

Not that she knew that, of course, but when the universe keeps gently dissuading you from taking a path, she knows from long experience it's best not to push against that too hard.

But now, with this stone, ways are opening once again and she catches a glimmer of the future: if she can fulfil this debt to Jasmari, if she can open up again the way that has been closed now for many years, a seed of hope will unfurl.

There is calamity coming, of course; the People have long known this, a moment of reckoning when all will be called into account, a time of change so deep and thorough it will wipe the very planets from the sky. Some seek to hasten this time, others to stay it; a bold choice either way, to Saefda's mind, since none know precisely what the change will bring.

But regardless, this, here, now, a tiny cuboid stone glowing pink in the hand of a human toddler... This is hope.

OUTSIDE THE WILLOW IN AIR COOLER AND DEEPER AND more oxygenated than the warm confines of her home, Saefda knocks three times against rough bark with one hand, then seven times with the other. Paces out the short distance counter-clockwise around a trunk she can almost hug. Whistles twelve high pitched notes, the callsign for the flock of sprites that she, as a member of the High Hall, is entitled to command. She hasn't called on them in months, now—not since the baby came to stay.

At her side, one hand clutched tightly in hers, said baby stands, fingers crammed into her sticky mouth, eyes wide and bright as she watches the tiny sprites, not much more than glowing green lights in the air at this time of year and month and day.

Well. Not so much of baby anymore.

Still, too much of a babe to toddle all the way to that place in the woods, so Saefda sweeps her up into a sling against her back, enchanted so that Saefda will feel no weight from her burden, and with a cloud of glittering sprites surrounding her, heads off to find the path.

Paths in the Realm are not like paths in the human world. Saefda has heard about their paths, about how they stay put, always in the same location no matter where you start from or where you intend to go, always the same length no matter how urgent your mission.

It breaks her brain a little to imagine such a place, how *frustrating* it must feel to be in a hurry and still know that your haste cannot shorten the length of the travel. It's almost enough to make her sympathise with the humans.

On her back, the child shrieks, a squeal of delight as she waves barely coordinated arms around, trying to catch the sprites.

Saefda purses her lips. Frustration is not the only reason she finds herself sympathising with humans more often of late, and she is not sure how she feels about that.

To have spent so long trying to distance herself from her heritage...

She shake her head, bites her lip, forces herself to come to a standstill and recentre herself before her thoughts lead her astray down a path she does not wish to follow.

Instead, she imagines in her mind's eye a fountain, issuing forth from a crack in the ground, rimming the underside of a round-topped marble plinth whereon is set... many things. A fat yellow candle. A white rose. A jar of clear liquid that swirls constantly without being touched and a twisted ring of gold that drags the eye around curves that seem to bend the laws of time, the sound of a magpie warbling rimmed somehow with frost and a ray of sunlight golden as honey, sourceless as the stars.

The rushing sound of the fountain drowns out all other noise, shorts out all other magics, protects the Portends from any would seek them who don't already know exactly where they are.

Saefda knows where they are, and more: she has the seventh portend, the one which will complete the circuit and allow Jasmari the foresight that she needs to know if her conspiracy theories about the dragons are correct.

Saefda doesn't mind much either way; the end of the world, or a world, or any world, isn't something she concerns herself with overmuch. Gone are the days when the Elders questioned her right to sit at the High Table in the Hall—but gone too are the days when she cared to answer. These days, she would much rather her willow than any great table. She cares much more about discharging her debt and avoiding any transformation into a personal supernova than she does about conspiracies, regardless of how juicy they may be.

And so, with mind set firmly on her desired destination—the fountain, the plinth, the Portends—Saefda gathers up her breath, checks with one absent hand to make sure the child is firmly in place, and whistles for her sprites to follow.

The moment she takes a step she knows both that the journey to the plinth will take longer than it ought, and that this is because someone is in the way.

And that is the frustration of the paths of the People: haste may often shorten the way to where one wishes to go, if the reasons for it align with the will of the world. But equally, in complex and chaotic ways, the presence of others influences the paths as well; to walk one path alone is not to walk it with company, which is yet another reason why Saefda prefers her remote forest home to the gatherings where most of the People live.

Well. Her path has transformed. So be it. She can stop, recenter, try to find another way—and the result may be just the same, so she decides to continue on regardless.

Scent bubbles rise around her, and for a moment she smells the salt of a deep, vast ocean. It makes her shudder; so much water altogether in one place, so utterly inhospitable to all plants except algae and kelp? No thank you.

A handful more of steps that feel nothing more than purposeful and firm to her, but which would leave the child yards and yards and yard behind, were she to try to walk along.

Lavender and thyme.

Birdsong, twisting and twirling around her, from all directions and none.

Her footsteps in the leaf litter, swirling around her like her little green sprites.

A breath of air strong enough to taste, of rotting fruit. Saefda wrinkles her nose. The scents of decay are not unheard of on the paths, but they are uncommon.

Sulfur.

Burning plastic.

Shampoo.

Saefda gacks her tongue at the outrageously human scents that cloy her way.

No wonder the path has transformed: there is a human here.

Mostly, Saefda is just irritated. Humans themselves are little bother, zonked out as they usually are, drunk on the magic of the Realms, insensible to what surrounds them. But that one should be here, now, today, to interfere with her path as she tries for the second time to reach the Portends? Saefda scowls.

The sprites huddle around her head, attempting comfort. She waves them away so she can see more than just their blinking green light. "Get back, give me space," she grumps.

They scatter, offended for three milliseconds before forgetting what they had to be offended for.

Whispers in the wind split the birdsong, overshadow the floating sound of Saefda's footfalls.

Goosebumps rise on Saefda's arms; the child goes still in the sling, as though about to cry.

Absently, Saefda reaches back to pat her.

"*Youv*," Saefda tells the path in the language of her People.

Obligingly, the path swoops upside down for just an instant, and when Saefda's next footfall lands, a man stands before her, body tense, hands clenched at his sides. His eyes are fierce—and smeared with green paste.

She recoils from the stink of crushed clover and soy. Recoils again when she spots the ragstone on the cord around his neck.

"Who are you?" Her voice cracks like the branch of a tall tree falling; he will have heard no voice, not now, not here; instead, the words will arrive wholesale in his brain, translated into whichever human tongue he knows best.

He smiles wryly instead of cringing in pain.

Saefda peers at him more closely, brow wrinkling as she examines his brown face—brown like the High People of the Hall of Wood, brown like the People who sit at the High Table. Why couldn't her mother have looked like *this*?

Unconsciously, she reaches a hand back to touch the child, whose skin is of a colour with Jasmari's. If she can just keep her safe for long enough to learn, the child might have a hope...

Of what? She can never *blend in*, no matter what she may look like. Ears, skin, height, eyes, it's all cosmetic and none of it can hide the fact that she is human, and the People will never accept her, no matter how hard Saefda fights.

Saefda is tired of fighting. Decades of trying to prove herself worthy, force them to accept her—and she's not even human.

The child?

Abruptly, Saefda is fed up with it all. She should have left the child on the road when first she found it.

She'll never bring herself to put it out of its misery, of course, but she ought to. It would be a kindness.

But there is a human here, and he is sane, and perhaps this is the better path for the child after all.

The man clears his throat and Saefda glares at him. It's as though he's been reading her thoughts, has seen the conclusion she's reached, is impatient for her to fulfil it.

Upstart little—

"I know of a place," he says, and his voice is level as one cut surface of the Rosa Fraenqa. "A place that holds something a friend of yours is seeking."

"Oh?" An eyebrow arches despite her contempt —or perhaps it *is* contempt. "And what would you know of the things my friends are seeking?"

The smile that thins his lips is wry, and complex, and far too knowing. "This will confirm her worst fears."

Saefda's heart knocks in her chest. What can a human know of the fears of the People? What can a human know of conspiracies too great, too complex, too vast for them to even begin to comprehend? Fury chokes her, and around her the sprites form up, an angry buzzing replacing the oxygen in the air. All around, the oaks and beeches, the maples and the hickory begin to susurrus angrily.

But Saefda is, if not as old as the true High Folk, old enough to know that often, anger is just a more comfortable coat to wear than fear.

And besides. The human is in her way, distorting her path. If he stays, the paths stay twisted here as well. She'll never reach the Fountain of the Portends in time.

She sniffs in disgust, taps one foot impatiently on the grass (tiny bluebells sprout around it where her magic has leaked out). "Fine," she snaps. "I will hear of this place."

He bows, briefly, politely. "I have information that will aid you. I would be paid for it in kind."

Saefda tuts but does not roll her eyes. "I will pay you."

"In kind?"

An in-drawn breath, a narrowing of eyes. In kind? This is no ignorant human, here by chance. Fine then. "In kind."

He bows again. "There is a land in the world of men—"

"And women," Saefda can't help cutting in.

A satisfying flash of irritation crosses his face. "Yes fine, alright, *and* women, there's a country there, Australia."

She nods. "I am aware of this land."

"On the eastern coast, twixt two great cities, a mountain rises to the sea. One: a dragon has crafted a demesne there." He holds a single finger aloft. "Two: a grove of haema glossia grows there." With his other hand, he withdraws something from a pocket—something that glints golden in the light.

Saefda inhales. She has no truck with conspiracies, but the golden, paper-thin, razor-sharp leaf the man holds between thumb and forefinger inspires a kind of awe she hasn't felt in a lifetime. She will not let him see, of course, but this is the kind of information that could change history.

"Three: he has already delivered fae"—she flinches—"magic to at least one human." The man's gaze bores into her with fierce determination. "My niece."

Saefda shouldn't care. Dragons are Jasmari's conspiracy theory, and chasing them with her only alienated Saefda further from the High Table.

Of course, humans being given the magic of the People is blasphemous regardless, and if true, enough to call an army down on the head of the one responsible.

Saefda ought to know.

She breathes deeply, forcing away anger that may or may not be entirely rational.

"And now," he says, chin held high, "three pieces of information I have given. I would be paid in kind: I would be paid three times for this debt to be discharged, and I would be paid now, before the minutes wane."

Oh ho, a human who indeed knows how to play! Saefda's lips curl in delight. "And what three payments would you have of me, oh clever one?"

His gaze is steady, his voice firm. "My child, safe passage in body and mind for both of us back to a location in the human world from which we may travel safely and easily as humans define this to our home, and an oath that none of the fae"— Saefda flinches, but he is unapologetic—"will bother us again."

His child.

His child.

So that is who he is, and why he's here.

Saefda narrows her eyes. "If I am to understand rightly," she says, leaning back, lifting her chin, unable to stop herself from shifting to shield the child from his view, "you are the one who entangled yourself with the People in the first place. It is none of mine that you consented to a bargain you now regret."

His face tightens. "Entrapment is a violation of consent."

She shrugs. "Maybe in your world. Still." Still. Hadn't she all but decided just now that the child could never survive here? And maybe...

Her jaw twitches violently for a moment.

...Maybe, despite it all, she wants the child to survive.

Maybe she even wants the child to have a kinder youth than she did.

She juts her chin. "Lucky for you, Iden Kumar"— to his credit, the way he tenses when she reveals that she knows most of his real name is virtually invisible, were she not watching for it—"it was not my Hall you tangled with. Unlucky for you, I cannot speak for the other Halls, but know this: you will have your child, you will both have the passage you require, and I give you my solemn oath that none of *my* Hall will bother you, now or into the future." And if any other Hall tangles with the child, they will have Hell to pay. "Is that sufficient to release my debt?"

He inclines his head. "It is." He holds his arms out for the child, the tension at the corner of his lips, his eyes, betraying his fear of betrayal. But he need have no fear: surely he knows, if he has come this far, that the word of the People is binding.

"Who waits for you at home with love?"

The fear deepens in his eyes, but he holds himself tall and straight as he says, "My wife. Her family. My parents."

"And who of these is most desperate for your return?"

His jaw twitches, once, twice. If he is here and in such possession of his wits, he knows why it is she asks: desperation is the easiest anchor with which to forge a connection between the worlds.

But if he is here, and in such possession of his wits, he knows the risks of providing such information willingly.

"You have my word I will only use this information as it serves to see you and the child safely home," Saefda says.

Some of his tension ebbs. "My wife," he whispers. "Jo."

Saefda nods. Not a complete answer, but it will serve.

She reaches around, lets down the sling from her back. Sets the child upright on the ground.

The child blinks up at the man, little brow furrowed, eyes wide, one handful of fingers in her mouth.

The man takes a step toward her.

Instinctively, the child moves a little behind Saefda's leg, hand reaching up to find Saefda's.

The man does not say anything. He does not have to.

It was not only Saefda's trustworthiness that he feared.

He crouches down to the child's eye level, smiles a gentle smile that is almost sufficient to hide his grief, and from his back pocket pulls out a small square piece of blanket.

Saefda frowns—but the child stretches out her arm for it before she could possibly have time to think about it.

"Buh-buh," she says.

Her father's smile loses its grief-stricken edge. "Yes," he says. "I brought you your bubba blankie. Would you like to come and get it?"

The child loosens her grip on Saefda's hand.

For just the tiniest sliver of an instant, Saefda holds on tight.

The child was an infant when Saefda found her, barely capable of feeding. How could she possibly remember a blanket? Hot anger crushes Saefda's chest—but only for a moment, before she shoves it firmly down. She has other, more important things to be angry about, if she cares to indulge in that particular emotion.

She doesn't.

That's part of why she's avoided the High Table for so long.

Maybe too long.

Maybe Jasmari is right.

Saefda releases the child's hand, and this time it's her smile that's tinged with grief as the child looks up at her, seeking reassurance or permission or simply just from habit.

Saefda nods. "Go on."

The child toddles to her father, who scoops her up onto his bent knee, and Saefda can see him wanting to crush the child to him, to hold her so tight she'll never leave him again, and for an instant she scents a future dark red with misery: but it will be okay, because although she can see the longing on his face as he tucks the scrap of creamy yellow blanket to the child's face, coos with her over it, says something that makes her giggle, Saefda can see too the careful way he holds himself, how he prevents himself from restraining her when she twists on his knee to gurgle back at Saefda.

He will give her space. They will be alright.

Saefda weaves a path for them back to the second world. First, a stretching out of her senses beyond the Realm visible in front of her to something higher, deeper: her connection to the universe, to the divine. Second, a rerouting, a lightning-fractal path toward the second world. Third, the search for desperation, the loudest emotion to those travelling the lightning paths, though love is the strongest emotion of all, which makes this two-fold easy, because she is searching for a connection that is both desperate and loving. In ways she cannot fully articulate, movements that occur on a level so instinctual she can no more control them than the digestion that occurs in her stomach, Saefda hones in on the streak of copper blue, the scent of gum-leaf grey, the rhythm of fingertips brushing with the barest of contact over a sandstone bench, all underscored by the complex, rose-scented, deeply layered sense of love, and the taste of desperation, which always seemed to her to be slightly left of citrus; lime left too long in the sun, perhaps.

She enacts a quiet braiding of possibilities in the air behind father and child, three of her green-sparkling sprites dancing like falling stars to set the magic to the path so it is, for a minute, fixed enough for those not of the People to climb aboard.

There. It is done.

Saefda returns herself to the present moment, the taste of lilies and cardamom drifting across them in one of the forest path's miasmas—and a reminder that her own path is calling her on.

Saefda purses her lips at the humans in front of her, still crouched together in the short grass. "I'll be watching her," Saefda intones.

The man's face pales as he glances up.

Good. Let him take it how he will.

Regardless, no harm will come to the child, not from human, and not from the People. Not if it is within Saefda's powers to prevent.

Grief knifes through her chest.

"Go, now," she says. "Or else stay here forever and rot."

She spins on her heel, strides off into the forest as maples and oaks tickle their leaves around her, and the sprites hover in the air above her, torn whether to follow their mistress or their playmate.

"No," she snaps at them, though quietly. "Come."

Behind, there is a rustle of leaves that lifts gently from the ground and floats around for a moment—and then an instant of utter silence, like someone has briefly muted the world.

It is the sound of the man and the child being swallowed by their own path, the magic of the People sweeping them away, erasing their presence from the Realm.

Saefda's own path explodes with light and sound and colour: glimmering greens and glittering golds, the scent of oxygen and sap, dandelions and tomato plants, the taste of hope thick in the air, underscored by the tinkling crescendo of birdsong that crashes over them.

She sets her shoulders.

Checks on the Rosa Fraenqa in the slip pocket of her tunic, the tiny pocket inside the bigger pocket where something small may safely lie.

Well. It's been nearly a year, but now the paths are clear: she will return the last of the Portends, and Jasmari will have her answers.

What Saefda herself will do about that, she doesn't know. Once, she would have also said she didn't care, but the man—Iden's—news has unsettled her more than she cares.

Perhaps it is more than well that the child has gone home. Saefda has a sense of a battle ahead—and perhaps she will return to the High Table sooner than she thought.

Once, she wouldn't have cared if dragons devoured the second world entirely.

Now, however, she has a steed in the race: she has a child to keep safe, a she will do whatever it takes to ensure that.

Whatever it takes.

Heaven help whoever stands in the way of *that* path.

About The Author

AMY LAURENS is an Australian author of fantasy and science fiction for all ages. Her fantasy novella *Bones Of The Sea*, about creepy magical bones and carnivorous mist, won the 2021 Aurealis Award for Best Fantasy Novella.

Amy has also written the award-winning portal fantasy *Sanctuary* series about Edge, a 13-year-old girl forced to move to a small country town for witness protection, the humorous fantasy *Kaditeos* series, following newly graduated Evil Overlord Mercury as she attempts to acquire a castle, the young adult series *Storm Foxes*, about love and magic and family in small town Australia, and a whole host of shorter works.

Amy also writes non-fiction books, often on various aspects of writing. Also dogs. Lots of dogs.

You can find out more about her at her website, www.AmyLaurens.com.

Read more by Amy Laurens!

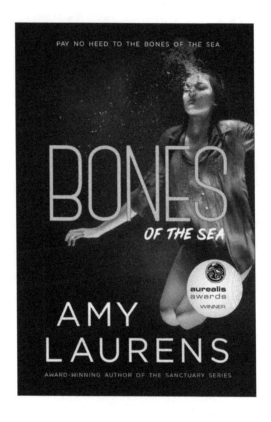

Available in print and ebook
from InkprintPress.com
and all major online retailers

Bones Of The Sea

THE MAN—WHOSE NAME IS IRRELEVANT, FOR HE SHALL soon be dead—wandered down the beach where sand whiter than any he'd seen before swashed between a short, head-high cliff to his left, and the frothing waves of the ocean to his right. Salt filled the air, but below that, something else lingered, and he couldn't quite place his... nose... on what it was.

Of course, the locals were horrified that he was here at all. But he was a Man Of Learning, and was not accustomed to heeding the warnings of people obviously less learned than himself, especially when they spoke tales of a beach that left no trespasser alive.

He'd scoffed. Ridiculous, their legends of a beach where to set one toe on the sand was to seal your own death sentence before the rising of the next full moon.

He was far more interested in analysing the sand, quite literally whiter than any he'd seen before, and thus far resistant to his attempts to decode it. He'd thought a pure variety of quartz before he'd arrived, but upon reaching the beach, pulling into the little deserted cul-de-sac dead end festooned with warning signs ('Cursed Beach, Do

Not Enter'; 'Beware The Bones Of The Sea'), he'd switched his engine off, opened the car door to the sound of waves and wind through the saltbush, and he'd seen the sharp drop-off down to the sand and had changed his mind to chalk, or maybe gypsum.

But there'd been no tiny fossils his portable microscope could detect, and the sand, whatever it was made from, had failed to fizz under the application of a drop of acid from his little glass vial, so that struck gypsum and chalk from the list of options.

Now, after several hours on the beach to no avail as the hot evening sun seared his hands and the light glinting off both ocean and white sand blinded him, he'd had enough. He'd run out of fresh water, ideas, and patience all, and was presently hiking back around the cove to his car that glinted silver and tantalising at the far end of the beach, a haven of cool air and fresh water.

Stay. Stay a little while longer.

The salt clung to his skin, filming his lips, the inside of his nose, the back of his throat. Somehow, the ocean smelled sharper here, more concentrated. Briefly, he wondered if that was the source of the townsfolk's rumours; but a higher salt concentration ought to have meant people floated better, drowned less. No. There must simply be a convergence of factors that meant the currents here were particularly treacherous, and indeed, casting his gaze out to the distant horizon, examining the interplay of wave and off-white foam, the cove did seem to be quite swirly, with a few smooth tracts he thought were probably rips.

As ever, folklore had a logical series of explanations behind it.

Just a little longer.

His leather sandal caught on something in the sand.

He stumbled.

Ow. That hurt.

Whatever it was, it had poked through the holes in his footwear to stab at his toes.

Glaring, impatient, our nameless victim kicked away some of the strange, defiant white sand—and inhaled sharply.

Once the initial burst of adrenalin subsided—something a surprise human skull will inevitably inspire, regardless of one's general composure—it seemed obvious.

Of course. The one thing he hadn't tested for was bone.

So focused on unlocking the mystery of the sand's composition was he that his initial reaction was deep, gleeful satisfaction.

Dawning understanding, however, made him lift his feet, hesitantly at first, shaking the white sand—bone—sand, think of it as sand, it's safer that way—but it's bone, really it's bone, it's all bone, every single grain of it, pure white, sun-bleached bone, spat up from the guts of the ocean the way a predatory owl spits out the bones of its prey—and then his feet were dancing, just like his stomach, as he leapt for the cliff and tried to haul himself up and off the beach because God, oh God, he was standing on bones and only bones, and the skull he'd uncovered had been human, and there, just down the beach, that rock wasn't a rock, it was another skull, and oh God, how many people had died here?

He realised the sobbing was his, rasps of panic as he scrabbled at the embankment that should have been easier to climb than it was, his fingers digging at the rock, skin tearing, sandals scraping for purchase...

Stay.

His back was to the ocean when the freak wave rose, a local tsunami of salt and hunger.

It smashed into him.

As it dragged him out to sea, all he felt was cold, so bitter it froze his bones right in his body.

An hour later, as the sun spilled red-orange life-blood out over the ocean, the ocean spat a skull, bleached-white and grinning, back up onto the beach. A moment later, as the full moon crested over the craggy headland behind, a sternum—*most* of its ribs still attached—joined the skull, followed a moment later by a single scapula.

And as the moon rose and the ocean swallowed the sun, a whisper began that sounded like the wind... until you realised there was nothing but saltbush for the wind to disturb, and the whispers sounded strangely like a voice, hungry, crooning, and singing.

Feed me.

Feeed mee.

Feeeed meeeeee....

Keep reading! Head to
inkprintpress.com/amylaurens/
bonesofthesea/
to buy your copy now!

Milton Keynes UK
Ingram Content Group UK Ltd.
UKHW010806220424
441551UK00001B/3